BILLIONAIRE'S SECRET BABY

A Second Chance Romance (Irresistible Brothers Book 7)

SCARLETT KING
MICHELLE LOVE

CONTENTS

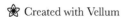 Created with Vellum

BLURB

**Being a billionaire stirred something deep in my soul
like nothing else.
But that was until I saw her again.
Her smile – sweet and forbidden**

My eldest brother prohibited me from making any scandal to
our resort.
I had learned how to turn my sexual prowess down a few
notches.
But in my free time, I did whatever pleased me.
There she is — exactly the way I remember her.
One thing's different, though.
The little girl holding her hand, calling her Momma.
Our eyes meet, sparks of recognition light in hers.
My heart flutters inside my chest.
Wait — what the hell.

**Does she think I haven't recognized the only woman
I've ever come close to falling in love with?**

CHAPTER 1
COHEN

Good financial news never failed to stir something deep in my soul. Money always moved me in ways nothing else could.

Whistling a happy tune as I sauntered down the hallway after leaving my office, I winked at one of the maids as she pushed her cart, coming my way. "Mornin' Miss Sara. Hope you're having a lovely day."

"The same to you, Mr. Nash." Her smile – sweet and genuine – told me that she liked her job at Whispers Resort and Spa.

Pride filled me. I did not doubt that our employees felt comfortable, safe, and happy with their jobs at the resort my brothers and I had built from the ground up. So, I thought I might let her in on something. "I'm on my way to meet with my brothers. If things go right, everyone will be getting a raise."

Her dark eyes brightened as a smile curved her plump lips. "Really, sir?"

"Really." We'd made a fantastic profit in the last quarter, and we always shared the wealth with those who'd helped us make it. "Your next paycheck should be a bit higher."

"Thank you so much, Mr. Nash." She hugged herself as if she'd gotten chill bumps. "I can't tell you how much I love working here. You're the best bosses anyone could ever ask for."

"Aww, thanks." Flattery far from offended me. "See you later, Miss Sara."

"See you later, sir."

Shoving my hands into the pockets of my Tom Ford slacks, I caught my reflection in a decorative mirror that hung on the wall. *Me, in a three-piece suit. Who would've guessed?*

Not many years had passed since my brothers and I had left our hometown of Houston, Texas, to come to Austin and build our dream.

I wore jeans and t-shirts back then. Since opening the resort, we'd all upped our fashion game. These days, our work uniforms consisted of expensive suits and ties. We wanted to make sure we made a statement that our resort was just as luxurious as our advertisements claimed. And that statement started with us.

I'd never looked better. Unfortunately, it was wasted on the women at the resort. Before we'd even begun the hiring process, Baldwyn, the eldest of us all, had sat me down to inform me that I wasn't to touch any of the women we hired to work at the resort.

I would've been offended had I not been sure that he was right for having the sit-down chat with me. I'd left my first few jobs after having short relationships with co-workers. The last job in Houston was managing a small hotel where I'd secretly begun dating three of the employees. I knew we'd be leaving soon, and I'd thought, *what the hell?* And I went for it.

So, I'd had my last hurrah and was ready to become a good owner with solid moral fiber — at least while I was at work. My free time was my own time, and I did whatever I damn well pleased.

I did keep it discreet, though. Baldwyn had also warned me

not to bring any scandal to our resort. He was right to tell me that too. For some reason, scandals had never bothered me. I didn't care what other people thought — never had. But I wasn't in this alone anymore. The resort wasn't just mine. It belonged to all five of us, so I had to learn to care what people thought, and I'd had to learn how to turn my sexual prowess down a few notches.

"This is so exciting, Momma!" I heard a little girl say, her high voice filled with enthusiasm as she stepped off the elevator. "Our room's so beautiful! I can't believe this is real life. Can you?"

The woman who came out of the elevator behind the kid stole my complete attention. "I *can* believe this is real life, honey. And I'm glad I picked you to share this amazing trip with." She flipped her head to one side, her long blonde ponytail resting across one shoulder.

I know her.

Striding through the lobby with a few people meandering around in it, I couldn't take my eyes off the woman. She was only about five-six or so in height, and her build was pretty average. She had normal curves for a woman in her mid-twenties — which is what I gauged her to be.

Wearing a comfortable pink jogging ensemble and white running shoes, I figured she was about to go for a run on our state-of-the-art jogging trail that went all the way around the resorts' grounds.

When I pulled my eyes off her to look at the kid whose hand she took, I saw she was dressed in the exact same outfit as her mother. She was her spitting image, only the kid had long dark hair in a ponytail that hung down to the middle of her back.

They made their way to the double glass doors at the lobby's entrance as I kept moving toward them. The woman looked over her shoulder before walking out, and our eyes met.

After a fleeting spark lit up her golden eyes, she dropped

3

her head and hurried to get out the door. But my memory had finally caught up with me. "Ember?" I called out. "Ember Wilson, is that you?"

She froze in place, her eyes on the floor. But the golden eyes of the little girl whose hand she held turned to find mine. "Who are you, mister?"

"I'm Cohen Nash." Reaching out, I placed my hand on Ember's shoulder to see if I could get her to look at me. "Did I startle you, Ember?"

Finally, she lifted her head and shook it. "No. I just wasn't sure I knew you, is all." She looked me up and down. "The suit threw me, Cohen."

Running my hand over the lapel of the suit jacket, I chuckled. "Oh, yeah. I forgot what I had on for a moment." Standing in the doorway, we were in the way of some others who were trying to get outside. "Come with me for a minute so we can catch up."

Nodding, she held firmly to the little girl's hand. "Sure."

Walking beside her, I led the way to the breakfast room so we could sit down. "What has you in Austin at my resort, Ember?"

She stopped, her eyes huge. "*Your* resort?"

"Well, my brothers and I own it. So, what has you here?" I took her elbow, gently urging her to keep moving.

She came along slowly. "I was given this trip to the resort by the company I work for. It's in the oilfield industry. I work away from home a lot and wanted to bring my daughter. But you own this place, huh?"

"Yeah." I could feel the tension in her body even though I had only touched her elbow. I had no idea why she would be so tense with me. "You okay, Ember?"

Jerking her head to look at me, she gasped, "Yes! Why're you asking me that? I'm fine, Cohen." The tension mounted.

So, I tried to take it down a notch or two. "No reason."

Leading them into the breakfast room, I gestured to the juice bar. I thought Ember could've used a stiff drink to help her relax a bit. But with the kid around, I thought that might be in bad taste. "You guys want some juice? I like the mango-pineapple the best."

"I bet I would like that too," the little girl said as she pulled her hand out of her mother's and went to the machine with the yellowish juice flowing inside of it. "Mom, do you want a cup too?"

"No." Ember sat down at one of the small tables.

I took the seat across from her. "So, how're things back home? Your sister doing okay?" I'd dated her older sister for a few months. Like all of my relationships, it hadn't worked out.

"Ashe is married now. She's been married for the last four years. She's got two kids, and she's really happy." Ember looked at her kid, who came our way with a cup full to the brim with juice. "You be careful not to spill that."

"I will." The little girl sat down with us. "You know my Aunt Ashe too?"

"They used to date," Ember told her.

"Oh." She sipped the juice. "Hey, this is good! Thanks for telling me about it." After another sip, she asked, "Why'd you break up? If I was her, I wouldn't have broken up with you. You're um, well, very um, well, I guess the word is hot." She blushed. "I mean, handsome."

"Thank you. You're a very pretty little girl yourself. I bet you have to beat the boys off with a stick," I said with a chuckle.

"You're funny," she said, then took another sip.

"Drink your juice, honey. We've got to get to our run, you know." Ember ran her hand through her daughter's ponytail, and I saw her hand shaking as she did it.

I couldn't figure out why Ember hadn't told her kid how we used to date too. The fact was that Ember was the only girl who'd ever dumped me. She couldn't get over the fact that I'd dated her sister first.

It wasn't like I went from one sister to the other. Half a year had passed between the time I dated Ashe and the time Ember and I ran into each other at a local mall and ended up in bed together later that night.

It didn't end there either. I liked Ember. She and I laughed at the same things. We liked the same kind of music — hard rock — and we liked the same food, too.

I'd taken her out to eat at her favorite restaurant, Red Lobster, on our first date. It was the annual Lobsterfest, and she'd pigged out. I loved the fact that she ate as much as she wanted without worrying about what I might think.

Ember could be herself with me, and I could be myself with her. Unfortunately, she broke things off after only a week of seeing each other. And we'd seen each other every single one of those seven days — we'd ended up in bed each one of those seven nights too.

Even though it had only lasted a week, it hurt and was confusing when she said we couldn't see each other anymore. She kept saying how her family would be so mad at her for seeing someone her sister had dated and that her sister would hate her. She couldn't lose or alienate her whole family over a guy like me — a man-whore.

I had to admit that when she'd called me that, it had stung like crazy. Not that I could protest since I was exactly what she'd dubbed me — even though I hated the term.

I suppose I still am one, though.

"How long will you be staying, Ember?" Even though she didn't seem to be nearly as comfortable with me as she'd once been, I had the feeling that if she and I could spend some time together, we'd hit it off again. And the idea made things stir inside of me that I hadn't felt since I'd seen her last — some seven years ago.

6

"Two nights is all. Tonight and tomorrow. It's a quick trip. I've gotta get back to work on Monday."

"What sort of work is it that you do?"

"Mommy works inside a little travel trailer with lots of gadgets that help her find out about the mud the oil rig is pulling up out of the hole. And she can tell if there's any gas in the mud too. She's a mud-logger. And they say if you see the mud-logger running out of their trailer and away from the rig, then you should run too because it's about to blow up."

"Wow." I couldn't believe little Ember Wilson would have a job like that. "That sounds very dangerous."

"It's not," Ember said with a tight jaw. "I use the mud samples to make sure that doesn't happen. I've never had one blow out on me yet." She tapped her knuckles on the wooden table. "Knock on wood."

Still, it sounded as if she didn't get to spend much time at home with her kid. "So, you stay in the trailer on the rig site — or whatever they call it."

"Yes." She nodded. "We work twelve-hour shifts, my partner and me. I take the nights, and Roger takes the days. There're bunks in the back of the trailer for us to sleep in, and there's a little bathroom and kitchen too."

"She's been gone as long as a month sometimes," the little girl said. "I miss her a lot. But I stay with my grammy and gramps, so it's not too bad."

Ember had yet to formally introduce me to her daughter, so I took it upon myself to find out her name. "Your mom hasn't told me your name yet, kiddo."

"Oh, it's Madison Michelle Wilson, Mr. Nash."

Wilson? Hmm, it seems Ember didn't marry the girl's father.

"Call me Cohen. Your mom and I are old friends, and I hope to get to spend some time with you both while you're here."

"Well, we've gotta get to that run now." Ember stood, reaching out for Madison's hand. "Come on, honey."

"See you guys later then."

"I hope so," Madison called out over her shoulder as her mother nearly sprinted out of the breakfast room.

I hope so, too — but the way Ember's acting doesn't bode well for that to happen.

CHAPTER 2
EMBER

How could I not know about Cohen Nash owning this freaking resort?

Seven years of making sure to never cross paths with the man, and here I am, staying in a resort that he owns. What were the chances of that happening?

Houston was a big city, but not so big that people didn't talk about each other, especially those who'd made a huge success out of themselves. And Cohen had made an enormous success out of himself.

I'd only ever seen the man wearing jeans and t-shirts — the expensive suit blew my mind. And he'd never looked better either. I hated how easily he affected me, making my insides melt just by seeing his handsome face. And when he touched me, moisture blossomed in my lower region, the way I'd only experienced with him.

Unfortunately, the way he made me feel was on the taboo side since he'd dated my sister before dating me. Not that anyone in my family knew about that one week of the hottest and most passionate sex of my entire life. And the secret week would have to stay that way — permanently. No one could ever know that Cohen and I had even shared so much as a single kiss on the cheek. My sister would die, and my parents would kill me if they ever found out the truth.

His wavy dark hair had been longer back then. Now he wore it in a neat, shortly cropped style that made him look much more mature than he'd looked back then. But his eyes were still the same gorgeous green as always. He'd always been muscular, but I could tell he'd devoted much more time to keep his muscular physique in peak condition. *Still the hottest guy I've ever known.*

Madison had already showered and changed her clothes after our run. As I emerged from the bathroom in a white robe provided by the resort, I found her sitting on the bed with my cell phone in her hand. "Yeah, Grammy, this place is crazy nice. And the man who owns this place knows Mom, and he knows Aunt Ashe too. Isn't that crazy?"

Rolling my eyes, I went to the closet to pick something out to wear for lunch. "Tell Mom I said hi."

"Mom says hi." Madison smiled at me. "Wear something nice like me, Mom. I wanna go somewhere fancy for lunch." She moved her hand over her blue dress, which made her dark hair stand out.

"Fancy, got it." I pulled out some casual grey slacks and a pink blouse. "I'll wear my pink flats with this."

"How about your black heels," she counseled me with her wise fashion sense.

"Didn't bring them." I was on vacation with my six-year-old kid; I hadn't planned a night out to town. "The flats will work."

"Anyway, Grammy, why did Aunt Ashe break up with Cohen? He's so handsome, and now he's got like a zillion dollars or something — at least that's what Mom said. Aunt Ashe really messed up."

"Your Aunt Ashe is very happy with your Uncle Mike, so she didn't mess up," I let her know. Plus, Ashe hadn't been the one to do the breaking up.

Cohen had been the one who ended their relationship. And as far as I knew, he'd done all the breaking up with all the girls he'd dated. He'd broken many hearts along the way.

From what he'd told me, I was the only woman ever to break up with him. Not that my heart hadn't been broken when I put an end to things.

I'd liked Cohen. We had similar interests, and I really enjoyed his company. And he had bedroom moves that blew my mind. Leaving him wasn't easy. As a matter of fact, it was one of the hardest things I'd ever had to do.

But it had to be done.

"Are you sure about that, Grammy?" Madison asked as she looked at me with raised brows. "Mom, Grammy says that *he* broke up with Aunt Ashe."

"I don't know why you care or why you thought that she broke up with him in the first place. No one told you that. You just came up with it on your own." I took my clothes, then went back into the bathroom to put them on.

"He doesn't look like a mean person, so I thought that it had to be Aunt Ashe who broke up with him. You know what she's like."

I did know how my older sister could be. But I didn't like my kid talking about her aunt in a negative way. "She's good to you, and you know it."

"Yeah — me and only me — for some reason. Not Uncle Mike, and she can be pretty mean to Abby and Joey, even though they're her own kids. You remember when she made them eat all the disgusting green peas on their plates? You didn't make me eat all of mine. That's because you're nicer than her." There was a pause, and then I heard her talking to my mother, "Grammy, I'm sorry. I know Aunt Ashe loves me very much. But she's very bossy most of the time. And she has to have her way *all* the time."

Looking in the mirror, I saw a line etched on my forehead. *I'm only twenty-seven for the love of all that's holy.*

Rubbing my fingers over it, I tried in vain to smooth it out. The fact was that I had a lot on my plate right now and for the last seven years. I needed this vacation to help take the load off my back for a couple of days. But now that Cohen was here, I knew that wasn't going to happen.

The man had a strong will, and once he set his sights on something — or someone — he didn't let up until he got what he wanted. And I could see it in his captivating green eyes. *He wants me.*

So, I would have to find ways to avoid him for the rest of our stay. And that was precisely why I planned on taking Madison out of the resort for all our meals. The resort provided all the meals for free, so the plan had been to eat at the restaurants there to save money. But with Cohen around, I wasn't about to take any chances.

The man was, and always would be, a man-whore. And I had no room in my life for a man like that. Actually, I had no room in my life for any man at all.

Since work already took so much of my time, my free time was reserved exclusively for my daughter. I'd taken the job three years ago, and it had changed our lives significantly.

We'd gone from living with my parents to being able to get our own place. Sure, I was just renting, but at least we had our own home. And I could buy my daughter the things she needed without relying on my parents for help.

Making good money was nice, even though it interfered with being with my daughter. But my sights weren't set on remaining a mud-logger forever. My goal was to work in my company's office one day — whenever a job opening came around. Then things would be different, and I would have plenty of time to spend with my daughter.

"Grammy! Don't say things like that. It's rude," Madison chastised her grandmother.

I'd finished getting dressed and came out to see what was going on. "Madison, don't talk to your grandmother that way."

Her jaw hung open, and her eyes were as big as saucers. "But Mom, she said that Cohen Nash was a no good, no account womanizer who used her daughter, then left her crying for weeks on end. And he seems too nice to have done those things."

"Tell your Grammy goodbye so we can get going. We've gotta go find somewhere to eat." I held out my hand, wiggling my fingers for her to give me my cell phone.

"I love you, Grammy. Even if you are wrong about Cohen. Bye." She swiped the screen, ending the call before giving me the phone.

"She's not entirely wrong about him, honey. But your aunt didn't cry for weeks, it was more like a few days. Her pride was injured more than anything else." The fact was that my daughter was right about her aunt. Ashe was bossy, and she did have to always have things her way. She'd always been like that. We'd gotten used to the way she acted, but Cohen never had. And that's why he ended things with her. He'd told me that much.

"What was Grammy talking about when she called him a womanizer?" She got off the bed, then went to look at herself in the mirror.

"A womanizer." I still preferred to call him a man-whore. "Well, he *was* one back then. But he was young, only twenty-two. It means he used to date a lot of different girls." Maybe he still did. The absence of a wedding band on his finger told me that he hadn't settled down with anyone. Plus, he didn't mention having any kids of his own, and I felt sure he would've done that had he had some. But what did I know? I hadn't even heard that he'd become a zillionaire.

"If he was young when he did those things, then I don't think it counts. Do you, Mom?" She smoothed her hair with one hand as her natural waves could be rather stubborn.

"You can't judge a person based on their past." Smiling, I took out the hairbrush. "Come here and let me give your hair the once-over, then we'll go find somewhere fancy to eat, just the way you want."

"While you were in the shower, I looked at the little book that was on the table. This place has three really fancy restaurants right here in the resort. I want to eat at this one." She ran over and picked up the brochure, then pointed at something. "I can't sound out the word."

"Essence." I didn't want to eat inside the resort and risk running into Cohen again. "I thought we'd go out to find somewhere to eat."

"But look at these pictures – it looks so yummy!" She stuck out her bottom lip in disappointment. It was a look that I could never say no to.

"Okay, honey. We can eat at the place you want." I would just have to make sure not to run into Cohen again. *Easier said than done.*

CHAPTER 3
COHEN

Closing my eyes, I leaned back in my office chair and set free the memory of the first time Ember and I had made love.

It'd been seven years, but I could still vividly remember it.

Her skin, the softest thing I'd ever felt, blossomed with goosebumps as I moved my hands over her naked breasts. Full breasts, even though she was only twenty at the time, they promised to grow even more as she matured.

And they have, too.

Her trembling lips were red and swollen from all the making out we'd done before she finally agreed to go home with me for a sleepover. I could tell how nervous she was to actually be doing this with me. "It's okay, Ember. I get it. You don't want anyone to know about this. I won't tell. I swear to you that I won't ever tell a single soul about this. But I'm only doing it for you."

"Thank you, Cohen. My sister can't ever find out, or it'll kill her." Moving her body in a wave as she rode me slowly, she moaned with desire. "But you make me feel so damn good that I can't *not* do this with you."

I rolled her erect nipples between my thumbs and forefingers. "You make me feel so good too, baby." I knew I wanted to keep seeing her. But I wasn't sure if she would be into that since she was so worried about her sister finding out about us. "Tomorrow, I wanna take you out to eat."

She stopped moving, and her jaw dropped. "In public?"

"Looks like you don't want to be seen with me." I had to admit that her words stung quite a bit. "We could go to the other side of the city or out to Galveston even. I don't want you to think this is only about sex because it's not. I feel a real connection with you. It's more than just sexual."

"Cohen, I like you, I really do. I've never had such a natural connection with anyone before. But this can't really happen. You know that, right?"

I knew she was worried about something that wasn't worth worrying about. "Look, you know that your sister and I didn't get along. Honestly, I could never figure out why she acted so hurt when I told her we needed to end things. We'd had this stupid ass fight over me ordering another beer after she told me not to. I'm a fucking man, not some kid who needs a woman to tell me what I can and can't do."

"I know how she can be." Her hands moved over my pecs as she looked at them while biting her lower lip. "How do you have so many amazing muscles?"

"I work out." I took her hands, pulling her down to me as I ran her arms around my neck. "Kiss me, and let's not think about anything but you and me."

"Agreed."

And that's how things went with us. We agreed on pretty much everything. Well, there was that one exception. We'd never agreed that it was the right thing for us to stop seeing each other after only one week of the best times I'd ever had. And I was sure it had been the best week of her life too. But she ended it anyway.

Opening my eyes, I thought I might remind her of the night we snuck off to the other side of Houston to go to Red Lobster.

Since it was nearly six in the evening, I called the head chef of Essence. He answered on the first ring, "What can I do for you this evening, boss?"

"I would like for you to make a lobster dinner for two, complete with the best bottle of white wine you have right now."

"Are you going to come into the restaurant to dine, or should I have it sent to your office?"

"It's not for me. It's for one of our guests and her little girl. You'll need to send it to Ember Wilson's room. And make sure you send a fruity drink for her little girl too." I hoped that would inspire Ember to spend some time with me.

"I'll have it to her room within half an hour."

"Great. Thanks."

I'd called her room a little afternoon to ask her to join me for lunch, but she'd said that she and her daughter had already eaten. And from the security camera in the hallway near her room, I could see that she hadn't left her suite since then. I had seen our staff coming and going, though, telling me that she and her daughter were spending the day getting pampered with massages, facials, and manicures.

I was starting to think that Ember didn't want to be out and about in the resort for fear she'd run into me. If that were the case, it meant she was afraid of not being able to control herself where I was concerned. Which was great because I also had a hard time controlling myself where she was concerned. That's just the way it was between us.

There was her kid to consider, though, and I hadn't ever had to consider a kid before. But I liked kids, and her having one was in no way a deal-breaker. All I wanted to do was spend time with them. I liked Ember's company, after all.

Did I want to have sex with her? For sure. But I knew that was going to be a longshot with her little girl around. In the future, though, well, that was a different story altogether.

There would only be a little over two hours separating us

when she went back to Houston. I could easily handle the drive to go see her as often as she'd let me.

Something on the computer screen caught my attention, and I saw that the meals were being delivered to Ember's room. She answered the door wearing a white robe, looking relaxed and refreshed.

There wasn't any sound, so I couldn't hear what was being said, but I could tell it wasn't what I had imagined. She shook her head and looked aggravated as one line formed on her forehead. She pointed the porter back down the hallway, and he left quickly, taking the cart with the tray of food with him.

What in the hell?

Moments later, Essence was calling me. "This is Cohen."

"This is Sammy, the room service manager. I'm afraid the lobster meal you sent to Miss Wilson has been returned due to her daughter having an allergy to shellfish. What would you like for us to do, sir?"

"Make up a couple of plates of mac and cheese. But don't send them up. I'll come to get them." Huffing as I ended the call, I berated myself for not thinking about allergies when I'd ordered the food.

Locking my office for the night, I made my way to Essence to pick up the plates they had ready for me by the time I got there. Heading to Ember's suite, I sort of hated — yet loved — how butterflies swarmed in my stomach.

This is so not like me.

But that was what Ember did to me. Things inside of me that no one else seemed to be able to.

Mentally preparing myself for her reaction, I knocked on the door. "Room service."

The door opened quickly — already, agitation showed on her very pretty face. "I didn't order — oh, it's you."

"It is me. I brought something for you and little Madison." She hadn't taken a step back, so I wasn't sure what her intentions were. "May I come in?"

Madison poked her head out from behind her mother, a smile on her rosebud lips. "Hi! You've brought us something too. How nice." She moved in between her mother and me. "Can you come in for a little bit?"

"I can." I watched Ember's puffed chest deflate as she turned and walked away.

Although she looked less than thrilled to be stuck with my company, Madison seemed very happy that I'd stopped by. She led the way to the small dining table. "Over here, Mr. Cohen. Someone brought us something earlier that I can't eat. Mom sent it back. What did you bring?"

I placed the silver domed trays on the table, then pulled the lids off. "I brought our famous mac and cheese."

Clapping, she laughed as she pulled the white robe she wore around her a bit tighter, then took a seat. "Yes! I love mac and cheese. It's my all-time favorite. How'd you know?"

"Because it's my favorite too." Looking over my shoulder, I found Ember heading into the bathroom with some clothes in her hands. "I brought a plate for you too, Ember."

"I'm going to get dressed. I don't feel comfortable in the robe." She closed the door behind her, leaving me and Madison alone.

Madison didn't seem to have that same problem as she was quick to grab a fork and begin digging into the cheesy meal. "I'm not gonna wait for her. She always takes a long time in the bathroom."

Taking the chair across from her, I sat down. "Did you have fun today?"

"Fun?" She shook her head. "But I liked it. I got a massage, but it kind of hurt at first. And then someone painted my nails." She held out one hand, wiggling her pink-tipped fingers. "See. My toes match. Mom got a color she called nude. I call it boring. I wanted her to get red nails, but she said no way to that idea. I think Mom doesn't like to stand out for some reason. Which doesn't make sense because she's really pretty – especially for someone so *old.*"

I tried to hold back a smile – I guess everyone seemed old when you were six. "Maybe she doesn't want to stand out because of her job. She's got to be mostly working with men on the oil rigs. I bet that's why she's not into wearing things like red nail polish, even though she would look beautiful with that color on her nails."

"She would look beautiful! You are so right, Mr. Cohen."

"You can skip the mister part and just call me Cohen. No one except the staff calls me mister. And you're a friend, right?"

"Sure I am." She stopped, her fork hanging in the air as she looked right into my eyes. "Since we're friends, can you tell me why my grammy doesn't like you?"

"Well, I broke up with her oldest daughter. And she must've never understood why." I hadn't meant to get into this type of conversation with the kid, but I couldn't ignore the question.

"Did you break up with Aunt Ashe because she's bossy and always wants to have her way?" She nodded knowingly as if she already knew the answer to her question.

I didn't want to say anything bad about her aunt. "We just didn't connect well, that's why I ended things with her. But she's married with kids now, so she must've found a nice man who she connects with, and I'm happy for her."

"I knew you were nice." She shoved her fork into the mound of macaroni.

"I did too," came Ember's soft voice.

It was too surreal. He was here, with us. I'd never seen this coming. Now that it was actually happening, I wasn't sure what I was going to do anymore.

Cohen pulled a couple of wine bottles from the bag he'd brought in with him. "I'm not sure which goes with mac and cheese, red or white, so I brought both."

The food didn't tempt me — not even a little. "I'll take some red. I'm not hungry right now, so it won't really matter what color I drink." The suite had a minibar, so I went to grab a couple of glasses and pulled out a bottle of apple juice from the mini-fridge for Madison.

"Madison said she liked what you guys did today, but she didn't have fun," he said as I brought the glasses. "So, I thought I might take you guys to a cave tour tomorrow so she can have some fun while you're here."

Madison started jumping up and down in excitement. "Mom, say yes, please!" Her eyes were as bright as I'd ever seen them. "A cave, Mom! A real cave! We've gotta go."

"I'll think about it." I couldn't make any hasty decisions right now. There was too much at stake.

"That means no." She sulked, her lower lip pushed out to

make sure everyone clearly understood that she wasn't happy with my decision.

"It doesn't mean no," I corrected her as I so often had to when I said those words she hated to hear. "It just means that I need to think about it."

"It's just a little trip to a cave, and then maybe we could grab lunch somewhere like," Cohen drummed his fingers on the table, "Cheesy Town Pizza and Arcade Parlor?"

"Holy smokes! Mom!" She jumped out of her chair and hugged me as if that might make me say yes. "Please!"

I looked at Cohen, who smiled sexily at me. "Yeah, please."

"I said I'll think about it. Okay, you two?" I picked up the bottle of red wine he'd opened. "You want a glass too?"

"You bet." He turned his attention to Madison. "That sure looks yummy."

She grabbed the other fork and handed it to him. "There's way too much for just me. We can share."

His grin gave his hunger away, and he was quick to take the fork, plunging it into the heaping mound of mac and cheese. "I wasn't kidding when I said this is my favorite too. My mouth's been watering ever since I picked it up."

As I finished filling two glasses with the wine, I looked up to find them both tilting their heads to the right. They were holding their forks the same way, too, and then they even chewed slowly and closed their eyes with identical expressions, as if the macaroni was the best thing they'd ever tasted.

How can she be so much like him when she's never even met him before?

"This is the best mac and cheese I've ever tasted, Cohen." She looked at me. "I wish you could make it this way."

"Me too. But the box I use probably doesn't come close to comparing to that recipe. Maybe your new friend could ask the chef for the recipe for me." I took a sip of the wine and found it unbelievably delicious. "Wow. This must've cost a fortune."

"A small one." Cohen gave me a nod. "And I can get you any recipe you like."

"She's never home enough to make it for me." Madison picked up the bottle of juice and tried to open it but couldn't. I was just about to reach out for it when she handed it to Cohen. "Can you open this for me, please?"

"Sure, sweetie." He opened the bottle then gave it back to her before looking at me. "You're really away from home that much, Ember?"

"I work a lot, yeah." It wasn't like I had any control over my schedule. "When my partner and I are given a job, we have to stay on it until the oil well is finished. The company men don't like any changes of any kind in the crew on their rigs. It's just how they do things. Most of the jobs only last a couple of weeks. But every now and then, there's one that lasts a month, sometimes even longer. But my boss tries his best not to put me on those. Roger's in his sixties, and I'm a mother, so he tries to put us on jobs that aren't expected to last much longer than two weeks."

Madison shrugged. "All I know is that sometimes Momma gets home for only a couple of days, and then she has to leave again. I don't like that. I think she should have as much time at home as she does at work."

"Well, this job doesn't work that way, honey. And it's a good-paying job, so I can't really complain when they send me back to work." I took another sip of the wine, hoping it would make me care less that she was airing our troubling family situation to a man who should feel like a stranger to her.

A look of concern filled Cohen's face. "Is this your career now, Ember?"

"It's a steppingstone. The company is rather small. I'm waiting for a position in the office to open up, and then I'll see if I can get a desk job where I can be home every day." Of course, Madison had left that part out while she was telling him all about how much I wasn't at home with her.

"Well, that's good. Isn't it, Madison?"

Another shrug. "I don't know when that's going to happen. It's been forever already."

"Three years," I said, feeling more than a little ashamed of how my kid was making her life sound. "And she stays with my parents while I'm away. She's got her own bedroom full of toys over there. This kid has it good. Don't let her make you think otherwise."

"I don't think she has it bad at all," he said with a smile that told me he was being honest. "I think she just misses her momma."

"Well, I'm here right now, kiddo. So, what do you want to do with the rest of our night? We could go see that movie you've been asking about. The one where the kids go to outer space."

"I already saw it with Gramps." She looked at Cohen. "What are you gonna do tonight?"

He looked at me. "I'm free."

I wasn't about to let him take us out both that night and the next day too. "Well, as my daughter has so eloquently pointed out, we don't get much time together, so I'd like to do something just me and her. You understand, don't you?"

Nodding, he looked a bit disappointed. "Yeah, you're right. You two spend the night together. I can hang out with you guys tomorrow."

"Can he, Mom?" Her eyes stared daggers into mine, daring me to tell her no.

I had no idea why she liked him so much. She hadn't had enough time to get to know him at all. I supposed it was due to his charm and good looks. The man must've emitted pheromones that pulled women of all ages to him like a tractor beam.

What Madison didn't know about the man was how easily he could move from one woman to the next without looking back. Sure, he'd spend some time with us, but once we left, we'd be out of his mind, and he'd move on to the next in line.

I know that all too well.

I had been the one to end things between us. But he'd moved on within a couple of months and never tried to get back in touch.

That had hurt worse than the night we'd actually broken up. He had no idea that I'd seen him holding hands with some other woman as they walked into a nightclub only two months after our breakup.

He was out on the town, and I was going out of my mind. He'd moved on, and my life had all but stopped. He had a bright future, and mine had never looked so uncertain.

With Cohen Nash unaware of how shattered I had felt after our breakup, he was capable of getting on with his life and new romantic pursuits. But romance for me had been put on hold — for what seemed would be a hell of a long time.

"Ember, you okay?" he asked, touching my hand, which was lying on the table next to my glass of wine.

Just like it always had, lightning ripped right through me with his touch. I looked into his green eyes, finding that the thin trails of brown still ran through them and around the outer edges of his irises. "I'm fine." I was more than fine as feeling his touch again made my heart soar. My soul begged for more.

"So, how about tomorrow?" He moved the tips of his fingers lightly over the back of my hand. "My treat. The whole day and even the night if you two want. I'd love to show you around and help Madison find some fun."

Finding fun was sort of his thing. Part of his charm was how inventive he could be when showing a girl a good time. Not that I had ever needed anything more than just being with him. It didn't matter where we were or what we were doing for that one week we were together. It was always fun, interesting, and sometimes even mind-blowing.

But one day with him would only end up hurting me more than I'd already been hurt by the man – even though he was completely unaware that he'd hurt me at all. And by the way my daughter was acting, one day would only make her ask me why there couldn't be more.

But there couldn't be more, and I knew that. Even if Cohen didn't understand or agree, my family meant the world to me, and I couldn't hurt them just so I could have what and who I really wanted.

The past was the past, but the people in my life would never understand the things I'd done back then. I didn't want any hard feelings with the people I not only cared about but relied on to help me with my daughter.

I hadn't done it alone, after all. When I came to my family, telling them of the pregnancy, they'd rallied around me and made things as good as they could be back then. Even when I lied to them and told them I didn't want anything to do with the father as it had been a mistake and a one-night stand. They'd helped me through the pregnancy and becoming a new mother at the tender age of twenty-one.

My sister had held my hand while I delivered my daughter. She'd been there for me in all ways. There wasn't a doubt in my mind that she would feel completely betrayed if she learned the truth.

Cohen had no idea that I'd followed him to the nightclub the night I took the pregnancy test. Finding out that we'd made a baby in the brief time we'd spent together had been very difficult. It had been hard enough having to end it after coming as close to being in love as I'd ever gotten, so I already was an emotional wreck that night.

But when he got out of his truck and went around to help his date, taking her by the hand and leading her inside for a night of drinking, dancing, and sex, I couldn't tell him what I'd tracked him down for.

I couldn't tell him that he was going to be a father.

And I never will tell him the secret I've kept from everyone for seven long years.

"I'm sorry, Cohen. I need to spend time with my daughter — alone."

CHAPTER 5
COHEN

I wasn't used to feeling lonely – it wasn't something I'd often felt in my life. Tonight was a rare occasion for me. Home alone, a glass of Jamison on the rocks in one hand, the television remote in the other, I was just about to plop down on the sofa to binge-watch something that would take my mind off Ember.

My cell rang, and I perked up, hoping it was Ember calling to tell me she'd changed her mind about tomorrow. I'd left my business card with my personal phone number on it on the table in her room to make sure she could call me if she wanted to. When I pulled the phone out of my pocket, disappointment squashed the hope that had so quickly welled up inside of me. "Tanya," I mumbled and sent the call to voicemail.

I'd seen her a couple of times in the last week. There weren't any sparks there, though. If Ember hadn't come back into my life, then I would've taken the call and would've probably ended up in the sack with the woman. *Sparks or not, some sex is better than no sex.*

With the fresh reminder of what great sex and a genuinely emotional connection with someone felt like – that someone being Ember – I couldn't muster the energy to even talk to anyone else. Tonight, being alone was better than pretending to enjoy Tanya's company.

Taking a seat, I took a sip of the drink. Although the liquid was chilled with ice, the whisky burned as it moved down my throat. A slow burn began in my stomach, not only because of the alcohol – Ember played a part in it too.

I couldn't mindlessly watch television with her on my mind, so I put down the remote and got up to take a walk outside. I'd lived the last year in the house I had built. My sister-in-law, Sloan, had designed it to my specifications and drawn the blueprints. I loved my home. But tonight, it felt as empty as a tomb.

With the idea that I'd be a bachelor for life, I hadn't built enormous mansions the way my older brothers had. Instead, I had a modest amount of square footage. The four-thousand-square-foot housed three bedroom suites. Each suite had seating areas, its own bathrooms, and enormous walk-in closets with private laundry facilities. I thought my guests would like such luxuries.

On the occasions when our cousins from Carthage, the Gentry brothers, came to Austin to visit, they'd stay at my place most of the time. Since I had no wife and kids to worry about, my place was perfect for guests.

Along with the spare bedroom suites, there was my master bedroom. My den of iniquity. I'd had my bed custom made. Larger than a California King, I called it a Texan Emperor. The head and foot adjusted with a remote control, so unique sexual positions were plentiful. And it was great for sleeping, too.

The home had a large living room at the front entrance. A chef-inspired kitchen — designed by my younger brother, Stone — looked beautiful but didn't get much use. I'd wanted Stone to have a nice place to cook from time to time. He loved coming over to cook up a meal so I could impress a date. He was a real wingman, my baby brother.

Meandering out of the media room, I went to the sunroom, then out the backdoor and onto the patio. The underwater lights of the swimming pool that filled up the large backyard made the clear water glisten. The sound of the waterfall feature echoed off the pale grey rock walls of the guesthouse.

Three guest suites were probably enough to accommodate my visitors, but a two-thousand-square-foot guesthouse out by the pool just seemed like a good idea. Plus, it had a games room that could be accessed right off the patio. A pool table, some old arcade games, and a foosball table were just some of the fun things to do there. A state-of-the-art sound system made that room home as well. It fed the many outdoor speakers that were all over the backyard.

Going across the patio, I went into the guesthouse. The lights came on as I entered. The maid service had come that morning, and everything smelled fresh.

As I looked around the living room, my eyes stopped on the fireplace. Turning around, I went to the control panel on the wall next to the door and hit the button for the fireplace.

In an instant, the lights above dimmed, and the orange and yellow flames danced within the glassed-in structure. Not only could you enjoy the scene from the living room, but you could also enjoy it from the dining room.

I walked around the house, wondering why I was even there. My melancholy mood had me acting oddly. Sitting at the table for four, I placed my glass on the shiny wooden surface as I watched the fire ebb and flow in a slow rhythm.

"Mesmerizing." The gold in the flames reminded me of Ember's eyes — light brown with golden flecks that danced at times.

As she came to mind again, I thought about what her little girl had said about how much she had to work away from home. There were things I could do for them to make their lives better. But Ember hadn't ever been one to take a handout.

I've got to figure out how to give her something without her seeing it as a charity.

A job wouldn't be seen as a handout. And if that job had perks – such as a home that went with it – then that wouldn't seem like a handout either.

Having Ember living in my guesthouse would mean lots of changes for me. Since she hadn't said a thing about our relationship in front of Madison, I figured she still wouldn't want to have a public relationship with me. And I was no longer the type of man who would remain hidden.

Asking her to work for the resort and move into my guesthouse could make things extremely difficult for me. With her living only across the patio, I wouldn't feel comfortable bringing women home.

Not that that would be the worst of it. If Ember was that close to me, then I would definitely want *her* in all ways. If she didn't want me or wanted me but not a real relationship, things would turn bad between us very quickly.

I have no idea what I should do.

Uprooting her and Madison just to please myself was too selfish. On the other hand, making it so they could spend more time together would be a genuinely nice thing to do. Although, she might find it a bit too generous of me and ask me what I would want from her in return.

And what would my answer be?

It would be a lie if I said that I wanted nothing from her. I already wanted lots from her. Lots of hugs, kisses, and screams of desire as we went at it like a couple of apes in the jungle.

She will never go for that. At least not the way I'd want.

Ember had ended what we had because she didn't want to ruin her relationship with her older sister. She didn't want her parents getting upset and disappointed in her either. From what I understood in the brief time we'd spent together at the resort, she still felt the same damn way.

Drumming my fingers against the table, I racked my brain

for ideas of what I should and should not do. I wasn't sure that Ember would even take any offer I made her. And Madison had to be extremely close to her grandparents since they'd been taking care of her for years. She probably wouldn't want to leave them either.

Taking another sip of the Jamison, I wished that I had the perfect idea. Or, at least, the self-discipline not to act on my attraction towards Ember if that was what would be best for her and her kid.

She wasn't alone in the world, after all. She had her daughter and her entire family to consider. I had no one to consider, and that made things easy for me. I could do whatever I wanted with whoever I wanted.

Yeah, but she could too if she'd only stop thinking her whole family would disown her for being with me.

Of course, taking a job from me and moving into my guesthouse wasn't going to be a thing any of her family would be okay with anyway.

So, why am I torturing myself with all these guessing games?

A smile formed on my lips as I nodded. I cared for Ember – always had. I hadn't even thought once about ending things with her back then.

The truth was that she was the only woman I'd ever started falling in love with. And she had yanked it all away from me so quickly that it broke something inside my heart.

The night she broke up with me was the second-worst time in my life. Losing my parents took first place. But losing Ember left a deep scar as well.

I couldn't help but want to see if we still had a chance at finding love – real, true love. I hadn't found it in seven years, and neither had she. That had to be a sign that we weren't meant to be with other people. We were meant to be with each other, and that was it.

How in the hell am I going to be able to get her alone long enough to talk about us?

I took another drink, closing my eyes to try and rid my mind of all the questions. This was useless. Ember wouldn't give me another chance. She wouldn't give *us* another chance. I had to come to terms with the facts and let go of the 'what ifs'.

Putting the empty glass down, I opened my eyes and saw the fire again. It didn't comfort me at all, as the golden hues only reminded me of her eyes and blonde hair.

I left the guest house and went to my own. Refilling my drink, I returned to the media room to watch television. I had to stop trying to come up with some idea that Ember would surely shoot down.

As I sat down, something came to me. *What if I get her sister's approval?*

Cocking my head to one side, I weighed the idea in my mind. *If Ashe doesn't care if we see each other, there would be no reason for Ember to balk at seeing me.*

Pulling out my cell from my pocket, I went to my social media app to look up Ashe. *You can't do this.*

I put the phone on the coffee table in front of me. If I asked Ashe anything about Ember, she would tell her what I'd done. And then Ember would be furious at me.

She didn't hate me, and I never wanted her to. I had no right answers for how to get Ember back in my arms and my bed.

Why does love have to be so damn hard?

CHAPTER 6
EMBER

"I wanna take a bubble bath, Momma. Would you make it for me?" Madison began stripping off her clothes as she walked toward the bathroom. "And don't make the water too warm like you do sometimes."

I'd done it once. "Yes, your highness."

After filling the tub half-way, I left her to her bubble bath and went to finish my glass of wine. I didn't drink often, but I wasn't going to pass up free wine. Passing the table as I went to grab my glass, I noticed the business card in the middle.

He left me his number, the little sneak.

I took the card with me then placed it in my purse. It might not have been such a bad idea to have his number — in case of an emergency. "You okay in there, kiddo?"

"Yes, Mom."

Going to bed, I climbed up on it then rested my head on the bevy of soft pillows. There were so many of them that they kept me propped up.

I hadn't let myself think too much about the time Cohen and I had spent together. It didn't seem like a healthy thing for me to do — mentally speaking.

But after several glasses of wine and my kid in the bath singing her little heart out, I had a few minutes of my own. Spiraling away to another place and time, I found myself lying in Cohen Nash's bed.

He walked in, naked and looking like some God. "Hey there, hot stuff."

A grin pulled up only one side of his mouth. "Who, me?"

"Don't act like you don't know it." I wiggled my finger at him. "I don't know how you do it, boy, but you make me insatiable."

Bounding to the bed, he bounced on it, making me bounce up too. Before I knew it, he had me in his strong arms, rolling with me, so he was on top, pinning me beneath him. "Good, cause I've got a never-ending hunger for you too, baby." He moved inside of me, watching my eyes as he did so.

"That feels too damn good."

"I know." He moved slowly. "I won't go too far without a condom on, but I had to feel you – the real you."

"You may have spoiled me." I arched my back as I bent my knees to make him move deeper into me. "I'm gonna go to the doctor in the morning and get on the pill. In a month, we can stop using condoms." I hadn't meant to say anything like that and snapped my mouth shut.

"A month, huh?" Nuzzling my neck, he nibbled on it a bit. "I like the sound of that."

Cohen Nash wasn't the type of guy who hung around the same girl for very long, so I had no idea why I'd suddenly made such a big decision. "Or maybe I shouldn't do something that drastic."

"You should totally do that, baby." Soft kisses moved back and forth along my neck as he moved his uncovered cock inside of me.

I didn't want him to stop. It was our third time having sex that night — our first night together. I had to think that maybe his sperm wouldn't be that strong since he'd used up so much of it in the last few hours. I knew I wasn't thinking right, but my mind was too occupied with other things – with pleasure.

Running my hands over his muscular back, I moaned as he moved like the waves of the ocean. The sex had been great before, but the connection I felt with him now was beyond my wildest imagination. I'd never felt this way with anyone else. But I hadn't had an uncovered cock inside of me before either.

The way he kissed my neck, the way he moved, it took me deeper and deeper into an abyss where there was nothing but him and I and the sounds we made — low moans, hard breaths, and the sound of our bodies slapping against each other.

He lay on top of me, his heart beating so hard that I could feel it on my chest. My nails dug into his back as my body began to peak. "Cohen!"

"Do it," he growled as his mouth moved up to my ear, filling it with hot breath. "I'll control myself. Just do it, baby. Come for me."

I couldn't help myself as ecstasy took over and I came undone, clenching his body between my legs, unwilling to let him move away from me as I arched, wanting him to join me in this bliss.

"Baby, let me go."

I dug my nails in even more. "No. I can't."

"Ember!" He pushed one of my knees away from him then slipped out of me. Standing by the bed, his hands shook as he took the condom out of the package then hurried to put it on his swollen cock. "Fuck!" It slipped right off — his erection was too big and wet from me to get it on.

He'd made me feel so good that I decided to do something to make him feel just as good. Getting on my knees, I reached out, touching his stomach as he dug through the drawer of the nightstand, searching for another condom. "I've got this, babe."

Looking at me as I ran both hands over his huge erection, he smiled sexily. "You sure?"

"I'm positive. Give me all you've got." Putting my mouth on him, I took him in deep, running my tongue along the underside of his cock as I moved my mouth over him.

I'd never given a blowjob all the way to the finish line before. For Cohen, I would, though. He'd shown me how great he could make me feel, and he'd done it as safely as he possibly could. So, I wanted to show him how far I would go for him.

A shiver ran through me as he took my hair in one hand, moving it away from my face and holding it back as I worked on him in a way I never knew I even could.

I wanted it – wanted to taste his juices more than I'd ever wanted to taste anything. My heart pounded as I let myself go – there was no thought in my head except his pleasure.

"God, baby," he groaned, "you look so fucking beautiful with my cock in your mouth. You've got no idea."

His other hand rested on my shoulder as I felt his body quake. I knew he was ready to let it all go. His breathing got rough, and his fingers curled into my flesh as he moaned with the orgasm.

It shot down my throat, then filled my mouth, and I hurried to gulp down the warm, salty, thick liquid. A bit more came, and I drank that too. I ran my tongue all over his diminishing erection before I pulled my mouth off him.

His eyes were closed as he turned then fell back on the bed beside me. "Fuck me," he whispered as he threw his arm out and grabbed me, pulling me to cuddle at his side. "You've just ruined me."

Laughing, I knew that wasn't true. "Come on, stud. I can't ruin a ladies' man like you."

"You have." He turned his face, and I saw something different in his green eyes. They were softer, somehow. "One day, I'm gonna marry you, Ember Wilson."

I had to laugh. "Oh yeah?"

He pulled me even closer to him, his lips barely touching mine, sending shock waves through me as he answered with a husky voice, "Oh, yeah."

Opening my eyes, I felt out of sorts as I returned to the here and now. My body shook as emotions threatened to take me over. I got up, unsteady on my feet, then went to my purse and pulled out the pack of cigarettes I kept in there to help me chill when things got too rough.

It was a terrible habit, and even though I rarely smoked, I knew I needed to stop – for Madison's sake, if for nothing else. My hands shook as I rummaged through my purse in search of a lighter. "How could I have put the cigarettes and forgot the lighter?"

"Mom?" I heard my daughter's voice.

Jerking my head toward the sound of her voice, I saw her standing just outside the bathroom with a white towel wrapped around her body. I discreetly put the pack of cigarettes back into the purse, placing them inside the little zippered pocket, then zipped it closed. "You're done?"

"The water got cold." She looked at me with narrowed eyes. "What are you doing, Momma?"

"Nothing." I closed my purse and walked to her. "Let me find your nightgown."

No one knew about my ugly little habit, and no one ever would. I would stop smoking soon. I just had to learn how to calm myself down without them first.

Being a single mother had never been easy. But lying to my entire family and all my friends was just as hard. And now I was lying to Cohen, and that made things even worse.

Guilt was stacking up inside of me now that I'd run into Cohen again. A part of me knew that he deserved to know the truth. But the fear of what that would mean overcame everything else.

Madison lifted her arms, letting the towel fall to the floor in a fluffy puddle around her little feet as I pulled the nightgown down over her head. "Mom, what are we gonna do tomorrow?"

"I don't know yet." I hadn't given it any thought, and that made me feel guilty, too.

"So, you have no plans for us then?" She walked over to her bag and pulled out a fresh pair of unicorn printed panties. "Then why did you tell Cohen we couldn't go out with him?"

I had no idea how to make her understand why I couldn't be around the man. "I'll make some plans before I go to sleep tonight, I promise. Now go get me the comb so I can comb out your wet hair. If you go to sleep like that, I'll never get the knots out."

"I like him," she said sternly. "He's nice. How come you don't like him?"

"He was my sister's boyfriend," I blurted out without meaning to.

"So?" She had no idea how things like that worked. "She's married to Uncle Mike now. She won't be mad at you if you like him now."

Well, she will be mad that we were together only six months after they broke up. And she'll be furious that I've lied to her for the last seven years about the fact that he's your father. So, there!

Of course, I couldn't tell my six-year-old something like that. "Well, I don't like him that way. And I came here to spend time with you – not him. If I'd known he owned this place, then I would've given the trip to someone else. I wouldn't have even come here."

Her head cocked to one side as she eyed me curiously. "Why would you have done that? He's nice. He's handsome. And he likes you. I know he does. I saw him looking at you with heart eyes."

I had to laugh. "You're such a little romantic, aren't you? Who knew?"

"I know heart eyes when I see 'em." She put her hands on her hips. "Colton from school looks at me with them all the time. I don't like him, though. But you could like Cohen if you let him spend some time with us. I know you could."

You're wrong, kiddo. I could love that man — not just like him.

CHAPTER 7

COHEN

I'd barely slept at all during the night. Thoughts of having Ember living right in my backyard had my sexual fantasies running wild. I did realize they were only fantasies, though.

If Ember took my offer, she'd bring her daughter along too, which would mean I would have to watch how I acted. With only a little over a month until my thirtieth birthday, I felt that it was time to start acting more like an adult anyway. And having a kid around might turn me into a better influence.

A man can hope.

With nothing to do at home, and since I was wide awake, I went to work early. As the resort's head manager, I'd had my office put at the very top of the building, on the fifteenth floor. Built right in the middle of the floor, I had an amazing view of the downtown skyline. A floor-to-ceiling window went all the way across the outer wall. I knew Madison would love it.

Since it was only seven in the morning, I had my hopes up that I would be able to catch Ember before she left for the day of fun she'd planned. I'd struggled all night whether I should offer her a job and my guesthouse. Eventually, my decision was made.

It didn't matter that she'd broken up with me. It didn't matter that she'd hurt me — all that mattered was that I'd cared for the woman once. Now, I had something I could offer her that would make her and her kid's life better.

I'd slipped a note under the door of Ember's suite, asking her to bring Madison and come up to my office before they left the resort for the day. I made sure to write that I had a surprise for Madison. I was fairly sure Ember wouldn't shortchange her little girl by not coming to see me.

I'd left the door to my office wide open, so there couldn't be any excuses about her not being able to find me. My name was on the door, but I wasn't about to underestimate the woman's ability to sidestep me.

Even after seven years, she must've still felt that being with me would hurt her sister. The idea was ludicrous — and I needed to make her see that for herself.

Getting to work, I had to put my mind elsewhere. A couple of hours had passed when I heard a knock. "Wow!" Madison gasped from behind me.

I turned in my chair to find her and her mother standing there, their eyes on the scene out the window. "Welcome to my office." Getting up, I gestured to the sofa. "Have a seat."

Neither of them could take their eyes off the view as they went and sat down. Finally, Ember pulled her gaze away to look at me. "You get to see this every day?"

"Not on the days I take off." Leaning against my desk, I crossed my arms over my chest. I'd worn something more casual, so Ember wouldn't get distracted by my suit. Jeans, a starched white button-down, and cowboy boots made me more approachable — or so I hoped.

She scanned my body, her lips quirking to one side. "Look at you."

Holding my arms out so she could get a good look, I asked, "You like?"

"You look a lot more like the old you that I used to know." Ember looked at her kid, who wasn't listening to us as the view had her mesmerized. With red cheeks, she changed the subject, "So, what's this surprise you've got for Madison?"

The little girl snapped her head around, her mouth gaping. "Mom! How rude! We're not in a hurry. I can wait until he wants to tell me what the surprise is."

Chuckling at the two of them, I held up one finger then picked up the phone to call the ice cream shop downstairs. "Hey, Alaina, would you come up to my office to pick up a very special friend of mine who would love to watch you make ice cream this morning?"

"I'll be right up."

Madison jumped up — a smile that wouldn't quit gave away her enthusiasm. "I get to watch someone make ice cream?"

"You do." I thought she'd be excited, but she was over the top as she danced around my office.

"Woohoo!" With her hands on her little hips, she shook her body to music only she could hear. "I'm gonna get some ice cream! Yeah!"

Ember rubbed her temples. "Sugar? This early in the morning, Cohen?"

"She'll just *taste* some ice cream. Just a little, right, kiddo?" I hoped this wasn't another blunder like the lobster surprise. "If that's okay with your mom, of course."

Madison stopped dancing to stare at Ember. Pleading eyes begged her mother to let her have some delicious ice cream without even saying a word.

"God!" Ember threw up her hands. "Okay. Just taste it, don't eat a lot of it. Promise me, Madison."

"I'll just taste it." Madison looked at me. "How many flavors are there?"

Shrugging, I really didn't know. "Not that many. They

make different flavors each day. Nothing but the freshest for our guests."

A soft knock at the door had us all looking that way. Alaina smiled at Madison, knowing right away that she was to be her guest. "I'm Alaina."

Madison ran to her. "I'm Madison! And I'm ready to watch you make some ice cream!" She took Alaina's hand as if she'd known her forever. "And taste some, too. Mom said I could."

Alaina looked at Ember, who nodded before she took Madison away. "I'll bring her back to you in about an hour."

"Okay." Ember ran her hands through her hair, acting like she didn't know what to do with herself. "So, I'll just head back to the room and wait on her then."

"No." I walked to the door, closing it. "I wanna talk to you."

When I turned around, I found her huddled against the side of the sofa, legs and arms crossed as she tried to get as far away from me as she could. "About what?"

"What are you doing?"

"What are *you* doing?" Shaking her head, it seemed like she didn't trust me at all. "You have some stranger come up here and take my kid away. And I can't even believe how easily — no, strike that — how excitedly my daughter went away with that stranger. I know you probably don't know a thing about kids, but you should know that kids shouldn't start their day on a sugar high."

"Come on." I hated when people did that. "I bet you've given her cereal for breakfast plenty of times."

She made a weird sort of laugh that sounded a hell of a lot like a snort. "Cereal and ice cream are worlds apart, Cohen."

"Not really. They both have lots of sugar. And she's not going to be eating a bowl of ice cream." I didn't want to argue. There was so much to talk about now that we were alone.

Each step I took toward her had her squirming even closer

to the end of the sofa, but I kept walking to her anyway. I took a seat a few feet away from her to make sure she had her space.

"Cohen, I'm glad you thought about letting my daughter do something fun. But I can't help but feel like you did that only so you could get some alone time with me."

"And you're right." I wasn't going to lie. "Since we have so little time, I'm going to get right to the point. I don't understand what's going on here. You and I had a great time, and our connection was out of this world. I've never felt, with anyone else, the way you made me feel."

A smirk formed on her lips. "Sure, you haven't."

I let the remark go; I knew she had to have known that I'd moved on and had dated other women. "How about you? Have you ever felt a connection like ours with someone else?"

Her eyes became glued to the floor, and her face turned one shade lighter. It seemed as if she'd gone into shock. I reached over and touched her shoulder to draw her out of the trance she'd fallen in. Slowly, she looked at me then shook her head. "No."

That one word made something inside of me begin to glow. "Good. That's really good to know. I mean that, Ember. All these years, all this time that's passed, none of it had taken away how I felt when I was with you. My feelings never faded."

"Yeah, me too," she whispered so quietly that I barely heard her.

There were so many questions I wanted to ask. I wasn't sure where to start. Finally, I found a jumping-off point and went for it. "Do you think we could give things another shot?"

The answer flew off her tongue. "No."

"That was a bit abrupt." I didn't know why she would say that when it was obvious that we'd had quite an impact on each other back then. And it was clear our attraction was still off the charts. "You can't still be afraid of your sister getting mad at you."

"I can too." She shook her head as if trying to shake off the thought of her and I being together.

"You need to stop doing that." I moved closer, then put both my hands on her shoulders, pulling her around to face me, forcing her to uncross her legs and arms. "This is me, Ember. You know I wouldn't hurt you."

For a moment, she stared into my eyes. "I hurt you."

"You did." Again, I didn't want to lie. "But I'm not mad."

"Well, the truth is that you hurt me too." Her eyes cut away. "You never tried to come back. You moved on. You moved on very quickly, too."

She wasn't wrong. "Look, I was stupid back then. I thought the best way to get over you would be to get someone else under me. You know what I mean. But no one ever made me feel the way you did. No one compared to you, Ember. I'm not making that up just to get into your pants either."

"There's no way you'll ever get into my pants again, Cohen. You need to understand that." Her chest rose as she took a deep breath. "You and I can never be. It's best if you just accept that now."

Fat chance. "You'll have to explain to me why that is, Ember." Moving my hands off her shoulders, I rested them on my knees as I waited for her explanation. "And don't blame it on your sister either."

"I've got a kid now."

"Nope." I wasn't going to accept that. "I don't care if you have a kid. I like Madison. And I understand that you're a package deal." I hadn't meant for this conversation to happen yet. I hadn't meant to rush things with her.

That was one of my biggest downfalls — rushing into things with women. I didn't seem to be able to control my impulses. It was time I got a hold of myself.

"Cohen, you have no idea…"

I stopped her, holding up my hand. "No. Let's start over. I mean — let's start over with another conversation. I hadn't meant to get to this right now. You're a mother now. I get that. You've got more than just yourself to think about."

I got up and walked away to make more space between us. When I turned around, I saw something in her eyes that told me she was afraid of something.

Is she afraid of me?

CHAPTER 8
EMBER

Cohen was right. I did have more than just me to think about. I had my entire family to consider. Not that he knew or would even understand that. "Before we leave this subject behind because you and I both know that you'll come back to this very soon, let me tell you why we can't even think about giving what we had another chance."

Leaning back on his desk, his long muscular legs made my stomach flutter. He was and probably always would be an amazing man to look at. And I was sure that he knew that as he gave me a sexy grin. "I'm surprised to hear that you want to go further with this conversation, Ember. Please tell me why you think we can't give us another chance."

Running my hands through my hair, I tried to figure out how to say it best. "The thing is that I knew how you were before we had our week together. My sister cried her heart out over you when you broke up with her."

"I've told you how that all went down, and I won't take all the blame for that breakup. I am obviously sorry that she cried. I'm not a monster, after all. But she didn't act as if she cared that much for me in the first place. It seemed to me that she delighted in trying to control me — a thing she wasn't ever going to be able to do. Her crying was probably more over her own disappointment for not being able to assert that control."

He's actually pretty much spot-on about that.

"Anyway, what I'm getting at is that Ashe cried over you." I had to get to the main point. "She told me that she saw you only a few weeks later with another girl. And after that, she spotted you several more times over the next six months with about five other young ladies. And then you and I ran into each other."

Holding up one finger, he stopped me. "I admit I was with all those other women after ending things with Ashe. I was young, if you'll recall, only twenty-two at that time. And I was playing the field, which is perfectly acceptable for a guy or a girl to do when they're not in a relationship."

"Okay." I knew he'd think that way. "What I'm getting at is that there were a plethora of women leading up to me, and I'm almost positive that there were still many women after me."

Nodding, he looked into my eyes, confusion clouding his expression. "I don't understand what your point is."

"My point is that…" I didn't want to be mean. But I didn't know how to say it any other way. "You were and most likely still are a man-whore."

His eyes dropped as he stared at the floor. "Ouch."

"I'm sorry if that hurts. Now, maybe you can see why I'm not exactly kicking myself in the ass over ending things with you. I'm certain that you would've ended things with me eventually anyway. You just weren't made for one woman, Cohen. I knew that about you way back then. And I'm pretty sure I was right."

"How can we know if you were right or not?" His eyes came back to mine as defiance filled them, making them flicker a bit. "You're failing to realize how much I liked you. Ember, what I had with you was as close to being in love as I've ever gotten – then and since. If you'd given us even a couple more weeks, you might've heard me say those words I've never said to any woman."

Nodding, I could see the sincerity in his words. I knew something felt extremely special between us back then. But I'd also known Cohen's character. "You're right. I might've heard those words come out of your mouth, and you might have heard the same words come out of mine. But then again, you might've told me the same words every other woman you've ever dated has heard slipping off that delightful tongue of yours."

"Glad you think my tongue's delightful, baby." A sort of sexy pride was showing in his twinkling eyes.

"You were the best lover I've ever had, so praise is due." I had to laugh to lighten the mood. "Look, I don't want to call you names. And I don't want to rehash what might've been." He needed to know some of the truth. "The fact is that I've never even thought about running into you again. And, if I'm being honest, if I'd known that you own this place, I would've given the trip to someone else."

His wide eyes told me I'd surprised him. "You would've gone that far to avoid seeing me again?"

Nodding, I saw no reason to lie. "Cohen, it's not easy keeping my hands off you. My memories of how things were back then have sprung right back to the front of my mind."

"Mine too." Moving to sit on top of his desk, he sighed heavily. "The only thing that's stood in the way of sweeping you up and spiriting you away to some secluded section of this resort is your daughter. Otherwise, you'd have already been the center of my attention."

"You think I'd fall into your arms that easily after seven years, Cohen?" I had to laugh. Some things never changed – he still thought himself to be God's gift to women. "I've matured. I'm not easily enticed into much anymore."

"You've had a child. I know that changes things. And I have to say, I do believe that's the only thing that's keeping us apart right now. Which shouldn't. I can be a positive role model for Madison if you'd just give me the chance to prove it." Getting off the desk, he came to take a seat at the other end of the sofa. Crossing his long, lean legs, he eyed me. "All I need is a chance to prove that to you, baby."

"Baby?" I didn't like that. "Cohen, you can't slip up and call me that in front of Madison, so stop doing that."

"You used to like it."

"I used to like a lot of things that I can't like anymore." He had no idea what kind of tailspin that one word could put my life in. My family would freak the fuck out if my kid came back saying that he'd called me by the endearment.

"Lots of single mothers date, Ember. Lots of single mothers even end up marrying. Are you trying to say you have no inclination to ever date anyone? Or is it only me who you won't date?"

I hadn't dated anyone since him. I hadn't had the slightest will to see anyone since him. But I wasn't about to let him know that. "For now, it's only you, Cohan Nash. For more reasons than just the fact that you dated my sister."

"Yeah, I'm keeping a tally on the reasons." He held up one finger. "I had the misfortune of meeting Ashe before I met you. And," he held up another finger, "I've also been with more women than you would've liked. Which I think proves that you have deep feelings for me."

"I don't see how."

"Jealousy isn't something that someone who doesn't care for a person feels. And it is immensely obvious that you're extremely jealous that I've been with women other than you."

Staring at the floor, I didn't know how to respond to that. I was jealous — he was right about that. But I couldn't admit that to him. "Am not."

"Are too." He smiled knowingly. "I can see it in your eyes, Ember Wilson — you've still got a thing for me."

Shit!

Closing my eyes, I growled, "Stop looking into my eyes."

"Why?" He chuckled. "Because they keep giving away how you really feel about me?"

He had no idea how hard this was for me. I opened my eyes and looked right into his gorgeous green ones. "Cohen, my eyes may be telling you what my heart feels, but my mind controls me. And my mind knows that I can't give us a second chance. Not only would *I* be hurt now, but my *daughter* would be too. Surely you've noticed how much she likes you."

"I know. She's adorable. I just wish her mother would give me the same attention." He chuckled again, then sighed. "Look, this isn't getting us anywhere."

"I agree." I got up, meaning to go to my room to wait for Madison to finish her sugar-fest.

As I strode across the floor, I felt his hand on my shoulder. "Where are you going?"

His touch sent sparks shooting through me. My knees went weak, and my mouth began to water as my lips trembled, begging me to let him kiss them just once. *Just one time, for old time's sake.* "My room."

"I haven't even broached the subject of what I really wanted to talk to you about yet. You can't leave. Not until you hear me out." He pulled me around to face him, resting his free hand on my other shoulder. Face to face, with only about a foot between us, I felt the incredible attraction pulsating in the space that separated us.

Slowly, he grazed his right hand down my arm then took my hand in his. Pulling me with him to go sit back down on the sofa, I knew he wasn't going to ease up on me. Not even a little.

The thing about Cohen Nash was that once he set his sights on something, he got it. And I wasn't going to be the exception. At least, not as far as he was concerned.

It took every ounce of my willpower I had to force down my body's needs and desires. Cohen had no idea the hold he'd had on me – and still had.

I would be his forever. In my heart, anyway. He'd given me the biggest and best gift a man can give a woman. Sure, it hadn't always been easy being a single mother. But Madison was a gift. And I had Cohen to thank for that.

One week of pure pleasure, and now I knew that love was there on both sides — not just mine. Our daughter had been made out of love. Even if neither of us had said it at the time, we'd admitted it to each other now, and that was good enough for me.

"Ember, our conversation isn't over."

Nodding, I knew it wasn't. "Okay." I swallowed, knowing I had to tell him something I'd wanted to say to him since I'd first felt our daughter moving in my stomach. "First, let me say this to you." I gulped back the knot that had formed in my throat as emotions threatened to take over. "I want to thank you for that week, Cohen. It was the best time of my life, and I will never forget it. Thank you for being so amazing to me and with me for that one week. You changed my life for the better in that small amount of time."

If only you knew how much.

CHAPTER 9
COHEN

Ember was all over the place — calling me a man-whore one minute and then telling me how I'd changed her life for the better the next. To say I was merely confused just didn't cut it. "I'm glad to hear you say that. It makes asking you this a lot easier since I wasn't sure how you'd take it before. But now, I think you might be happy."

"As long as it's not about you and me, then I'm all ears." She crossed her legs, resting her clasped hands on her knee as she cocked her head a little to one side, for once showing interest in what I had to say.

I found that to be a good sign and forged ahead. "It's clear to me that you haven't been able to spend much time with your daughter in the last few years. I think I have something that could help with that."

"I don't see how *you* can help." The slightest flush turned her cheeks a light pink as selfish pride must've been percolating inside her.

I just hoped that wasn't anger beginning to simmer. So, I tried to make sure my words wouldn't offend her in any way. "As a single mother, I bet things have been rough on you — even with the help of your family."

Her jaw tight, she nodded only once. "You're right. Raising a kid on your own isn't easy."

Nodding, I went on, "I know the job you have now takes so much of your valuable time."

Uncrossing her legs, a frown formed on her pretty face. "Cohen, what exactly are you trying to say to me?"

Shit. I better figure out how to say this a hell of a lot faster before I piss her off.

"I'm in the position to give you a job here at the resort. That's what I'm trying to say."

"Why would you do that? And what kind of job could I do here anyway?"

I liked her questions; they made it sound promising that she might actually take my offer. "You were in college when we met. What was your major?" I felt sort of bad for not having asked her before. But our minds had been on other things.

Tension filled her, making her body stiff as she nervously played with her hands in her lap. "It was business."

"Great!" I could put her into plenty of jobs at the resort with that degree. "There're so many management jobs here, it'll make your head spin."

"Damn, Cohen. You didn't let me finish." With a quick movement, she stood then walked over to the window, pacing back and forth in front of it as she kept her gaze towards the floor. "That *was* my major. But I didn't get a degree of any kind. I was in my second year of college — not even halfway done — when I found out I was pregnant."

"Being pregnant shouldn't have stopped you from continuing with college." I bit my lip as she snapped her head around to glare at me. "Not that it's any of my business. I'll just shut up now." *I don't know what had come over me!*

Moving her hands to her hips, she went on, "I wasn't about to tell my parents about the pregnancy until I had things under control. I knew that I needed a couple of things. One being a job, so I could buy everything I'd need for my baby. And the other was health insurance to pay for the doctors and the hospital. I wasn't going to burden my parents with anything. It wasn't their fault that I'd done something foolish."

It sounds like she was all alone in this.

"The father didn't…"

She looked away, avoiding my eyes. "I didn't tell him."

"Oh." I had to wonder at that decision, but it wasn't any of my business, so I tried to keep my questions to myself. One slipped out anyway. "Was he that bad of a guy?"

"Cohen, please." Turning her back to me, she looked out the window at the skyline. "I didn't tell anyone about the pregnancy until I was five months pregnant."

"How far into it were you when you figured out that you were pregnant?"

"A couple of months." She kept her back to me, and I felt as if she didn't want to witness any of my expressions, lest they be disapproving. "For three months, I kept the baby a secret from my family and friends. I barely began to show until late in the fourth month, so it wasn't hard to hide it."

"When did you quit college?"

"As soon as I found out that I was going to have a baby. I quit all my classes before starting to search for a job that would give me benefits. And it wasn't easy. I finally got a job managing a storage facility. You know, the ones where people rent little storage units to store all their junk."

"That sounds pretty easy." I wasn't sure what to say. Ember was smart — too smart to have limited herself that much. "So, that got you through until you got the job in the oilfield?"

"It did." Finally, she came back and sat down, facing me again. "I make a good living now, and I have great benefits. I doubt you have a job here that can pay me that well, seeing that I don't hold a diploma any higher than a high school degree."

"Don't be so quick to jump to conclusions. You do have a few years of managerial experience. That could get you into something here, I'm sure. And you would have time to attend online college and get the degree you began back then if you want. That's a plus for you."

"While that sounds very nice, I don't think there's a job here that can pay me what I'm making now. I get almost sixty thousand a year. I'm guessing that anything I could get here would only pay minimum wage or just a little higher."

"You'd be looking at a forty-hour week here. I'm assuming you work a twelve-hour day, seven days a week, right now." I knew that was way too long for any parent to be working away from their little kid. "So, yeah, the pay will be less, I'm sure. There are no minimum wage jobs here, though. We pay on a higher scale than that. I can't promise you the kind of money you've been making. But think about what you'd get in return — time with your daughter. She deserves that, don't you agree?"

Chewing on her lower lip, it seemed to me that she was thinking things over. But then she opened her mouth and out came the words, "I get it. You think I'm a lousy mother."

Jumping up, I was shocked by the accusation. "No, I don't think that at all, Ember. Don't go putting words into my mouth. Your daughter loves you, and it shows. You love her too. And I think you're doing what you think is best for her. I'm just saying that I can offer you some things that others can't or won't. I care about you. Don't forget that."

"Come on, Cohen." Her shoulder slumped, telling me she had some pretty deep insecurities about the type of mother she was. "I leave my kid with my parents more than I'm home with her. You would be some kind of saint if you didn't think that made me a crappy mother."

"I guess I'm some sort of a saint then because I definitely would not call you a crappy mother. Not ever, Ember. God!" I threw my hands in the air, fed up that she was so blind to how I felt about her. "Can't you see that I fucking care about you?"

"You don't even know me anymore, Cohen." Her golden-brown eyes shimmered as if she were holding back tears.

Sitting right next to her, I pushed her hair back, away from her pretty face. "I know you, girl. I know you better than you think I do. And I know that guilt has been eating you up inside."

She closed her eyes as if trying to hide from me. "Stop. Please, stop."

"Stop what?" I wasn't about to just give up on her. "Trying to help you? Stop trying to make things happen so *you* can actually raise *your* kid the way you want? Stop being here for you?" Smoothing my knuckles across her cheek, I yearned to kiss her quivering lips. But I knew I couldn't do that — not yet.

Her lashes parted, and she blinked a few times. Still, she wouldn't look at me. "There's so much guilt inside of me. You're right about that. But what you don't understand is that *you* can't help me get rid of any of it. My family won't be happy to find out you're the one who's giving me this opportunity."

And here we go again with the family.

"You can't miss out on opportunities just because you're afraid to offend your sister. The fact is, if she gets mad over you making a better life for you and Madison — just because *I'm* helping you — then she's not much of a sister. And you know that."

"All I know is that I can't let you give me something that I don't deserve." Finally, she looked into my eyes. "I can't take a job someone else would be better suited for."

"I'll hook you up with our human resources department, and they'll see what you're suited for. Plus, our company pays full tuition for any employee who goes to college to further their education in any of the departments we have here." She couldn't turn this opportunity down. "After ninety days, you'll get full benefits. When you add in all the great perks that come along with working here, like free meals while you're at work and paid holidays and vacations, well, how can you not even think about it?"

Taking my hand away from her face, she held it against her chest. I could feel the way her heart was pounding. "You can feel that, right?"

I couldn't stop the smile from curling my lips. "I've always affected you that way."

Nodding, she agreed, "Yes, you have. And that's why this won't ever work. That's why I can't work here. That's why I can't take you up on an offer that seems too good to refuse. I can't be around you and not want to be with you."

Why is she making this so fucking hard?

"You think I'm gonna hurt you, don't you?" That had to be the reason she was turning all of this down — me and the job.

Laughing quietly, she shook her head. "No, Cohen. I think *I'm* going to hurt you. I can't — no matter how much you say that I can — see you in a romantic way. Ever."

"You mean that you can't tell your family about us — if you and I did start up a romance." I didn't like the idea of her keeping our relationship a secret, but I could deal with that for a little while. "Giving you a job is different. And whatever happens between you and I is *our* business and no one else's."

"I'm not alone anymore. I'm part of a package. And Madison couldn't know about anything we did either – I wouldn't want to risk her feelings. And there's no way she could keep it a secret from my family. I can't allow that to happen. So, there will be no *us*. And I *can't* take a job here. It's extremely nice of you to offer, but I can't take you up on it."

CHAPTER 10
EMBER

Nothing deterred the man. After his face turned to an unnatural shade of red — I must've frustrated him to no end — he took a deep breath. His naturally tan color came back, and he said with a calm tone, "I think I've forgotten about something that must be of the utmost importance to you. Forgive me, Ember."

"For what, exactly?"

"For not thinking about your family. I'm sure since they've been taking care of Madison for you so much of the time, that you're worried about losing that support system."

He'd hit one of the reasons, but not all of them. "There is that. But there's so much more, too. Can you imagine how Madison would feel if she left her grandparents? And my parents would feel terrible about losing her too. Ashe picks Madison up every Wednesday to take her to dance classes, and I'm sure they'd both miss that. You have no idea how interlaced we all are. I can't just pack up my kid and move her away from all the people she loves. It would hurt them all."

And I sure as shit couldn't tell them I was taking her away so I could take a job from Cohen Nash!

"I get that." He walked to his desk, opening the top drawer.

Taking out a piece of paper, he sat down at the desk then picked up a pen. "When I've got big decisions to make, I like to make a list of pros and cons. So, I'm gonna do that for you. Pros." He smiled at me. "The most obvious one is that you'd be close to me."

Leaning back on the sofa, I held up one finger. "Cons, I'd have to relocate."

"Oh, yeah." He put the pen down, steepling his fingers as he leaned his elbows on the desk before resting his chin on the little teepee he'd created. "About that relocating thing. I've forgotten to tell you about this little perk."

"Perk?" I didn't completely like the way that sounded. "Does the job come with a moving allowance or something like that?"

"No." His green eyes bore into mine as if he was attempting to use some sort of mind control to get me to do as he wanted. "I've got a guesthouse."

"Nope." *That's way too close to him.*

"Hear me out, Ember. It's got a private entrance and a parking area too. You wouldn't even have to see me unless you wanted to."

"Cohen, you know how things would go if I lived that close to you." I wasn't trying to fool myself into thinking that I could actually take the job. And yet I kept talking about it – and that was disturbing.

Somewhere in my deep unconscious mind, I must've actually wanted to take the job and make a life with Cohen part of it. But I couldn't do that.

Wiggling his dark brows, his grin mischievous, he said, "Only if you want them to, baby."

"What did I tell you about calling me baby?" My cheeks got hot as hell while naughty thoughts rushed into my mind. Waving my hand in front of my face, I tried to cool myself down. "See what you do to me."

"And I'm not even trying." Leaning back in his office chair, he splayed his legs out, placing his hands behind his head. "You should just stop fighting the inevitable."

"The only thing that's inevitable is that I'm taking my daughter and going back to our home in Houston tomorrow." There was nothing he could say to make me change my mind.

Sure, for a brief amount of time, the man had influenced my moral character in a way I'd never imagined anyone could. Cohen Nash had charmed the pants right off me. But only for one week.

I'd managed to regain my self-control and get back on the right path without anyone ever knowing I'd strayed from it in the first place. But it had always intrigued me how he'd managed to lure me in.

For a long moment, he sat there, looking up at the tall ceiling. Then he looked at me. "You could do that. You could go back home to Houston, and soon after that, you'll have to leave home for your job. And things could get right back to normal. Only it might not be as easy as you think it'll be."

"And what do you mean by that?"

"Well, this time, you'll know there's an alternative. And you'll know right where to find me. You've even got my cell number. And you'll be thinking — as you're driving to work and spending endless hours without your daughter — that one phone call could change it all. One call could change your life – and Madison's, too." He paused for a moment to let that sink in. "You should come over to see the house you're passing up."

"No way." Judging by his office and his wardrobe, the man was as rich as hell. I had no doubt that his home was something out of a dream. The guesthouse was most likely far better than that of my parents' — I couldn't put that sort of pressure on myself. And I knew damn well that my daughter would fall head over heels in love with it.

If something like that happened, it would put a world of hurt on my relationship with Madison when I told her that we couldn't take the job and the home.

The subject needed changing — and fast. "Hey, there's something that I've always wanted to ask you."

"Shoot." He began moving his chair side to side in a slow fashion, playfully.

"How'd you do it?" I asked.

"Do what?"

"Make me change my mind that day we met at the mall. There was no way in hell I was going to hang out with you that night. And then — in an instant — I changed my mind and went with you."

A deep chuckle made his chest move a little as he winked at me. "It was just me being me, Ember. Nothing more. I'm not magical or anything. You were into me, and I could sense that. You just needed to let your guard down enough to let me in. And boy, you did do that, didn't ya?"

Blood rushed through me, heating my core and swamping my panties with desire as the memory came back to me. "Yeah, I did do that. It wasn't like me at all. It was like I was someone else that week. It's never happened again. And I doubt it ever will."

"But it could." His deep sigh told me more than any of his words could.

He's disappointed in me.

I was the type of person who absolutely hated anyone being disappointed in me. I would jump through hoops to avoid that.

But I couldn't change that where Cohen was concerned. If I didn't disappoint him, I would disappoint my entire family. I couldn't do that to them, not after all they'd done to help me with my daughter.

As much as I had tried to take the burden of my pregnancy and baby off my family, they'd still bore a tremendous amount of it anyway. There wasn't anything I could do to stop it from happening.

You could've contacted her father and asked him for help. I hated when my conscience spoke to me. It was as if that little voice in my head had no idea who my family was sometimes. *I'll pretend I didn't hear that.*

Cohen opened the laptop lying on his desk and tapped something. "Hey, listen to this job that's available right here in this very resort, Ember." He laughed. "Imagine this; I've just opened this thing up, and there it is — the perfect job for you."

Without a clue why I was doing it, I got up to see what he was looking at. "I don't have any experience working at a resort – there isn't any job here that I would be qualified for." Yet, I still went to see what he'd found.

"You have experience in this." He filled the screen with the job description as I leaned over his broad shoulders, trying hard not to breathe in his woodsy scent deep into my lungs. I was too tempted to try to hold onto it forever. "Guest services – security division."

"I've never been in security a day in my life." I knew he was grasping at straws.

"Listen to the description," he went on as if I hadn't said a thing. "The guests at our resort often carry valuable assets with them when traveling. Our resort is equipped with a safe room where deposit boxes are available to store their valuables. This position requires great confidentiality and rigorous attention to the safety of all deposit boxes and their contents. Ensuring guests sign in and out, checking proper identification, and interacting in a professional manner are required. This position is one of great responsibility, requiring a high-security clearance, which is reflected in the salary."

"Are you saying that you think this job is similar to the job at the storage unit company?" I laughed out loud – he couldn't have been more wrong. "Cohen, those people stored their *junk* in those units. And I wasn't even in charge of making sure no one else got into them. They used their own locks and kept hold of their own keys. The only time I got inside someone's unit was when they didn't pay the rent, and I had to cut the locks to let the auction crew in to sell the junk."

"Ember, you *are* qualified for this position. You must've taken down the personal information of the people who rented the units. And you must've kept track of who had which unit. That's about all you've got to do at this job. Keep track of whose stuff is in which box, and make sure you only allow that person to access that box. And the pay is good too."

"I'm sure that's shift work. I'd probably get the graveyard shift, and then I wouldn't have anyone to watch Madison." *What am I saying? I can't take this job!*

"We've got an onsite daycare for all of our employees. Did I forget to mention that? It's open twenty-four seven. And it's free." He seemed to have all the right answers. "I happen to be a bigshot around here, and I can pull some strings to get you the morning shift so you'd have lots of time to spend with your daughter after she gets out of school. The daycare even has a bus to pick up kids who are in school."

"You have all the bells and whistles around this place, don't you?" It was like a dream come true. A normal day of work and a daycare right here — for free, even. But there was that one little catch. *Cohen.*

"We certainly do. That's exactly why I want you to come work here. It's a great place, and my brothers and I are extremely proud of what we've done here for both our guests and employees. I've left out another perk. We have a doctor here to see to any guests who might come down with something while they're staying with us. And the doc can take a look at any employee or kid in the daycare too. All for free."

"Free, free, free." I knew it would sound insane for me not to even consider applying for the job. But I *couldn't* take it. I couldn't stay anywhere near him. "The rent on your guesthouse must be pricey, though."

Shaking his head, he just smiled. "I'm not about to charge you any rent, Ember. That's a perk too."

Anger welled up inside of me. I was furious. Not with him. But with myself. I'd done all of this to myself. I shouldn't have ever slept with my sister's ex. I shouldn't have had unprotected sex of any kind with him. And I shouldn't have come to the damn resort that would stir up so much of my past.

"Free?" I growled through gritted teeth. "Nothing comes free. I'm not an idiot, you know. I can see right through you, Cohen Nash. You mean to keep me around just so you can play with me whenever you get the urge. Well, that's not gonna happen, buddy."

Storming out of his office, knowing I didn't mean those ugly words, I held back the sobs hanging heavy inside my chest.

CHAPTER 11
COHEN

Something much deeper was going on with Ember — I just didn't know what it was. The way she'd stormed out of my office made no sense.

Sure, I hadn't stopped playing the field, and I knew I should've by now. But I didn't use women as playthings — I never had. I respected my partners and made sure we both had a fun time. I never made false promises. I just lived life by my own rules. That meant I could do whatever I wanted — even settle down with the right woman when the time came.

Losing my parents when I was eleven had had a profound effect on me. I knew all of my brothers had processed it differently, and it had done something to me that it hadn't done to the rest of them. Maybe it was because I was almost an adolescent, but their deaths had made me see that life was fleeting. Mom and Dad were there one morning — I went to my sixth-grade class like every other morning. A bit later, my teacher, Mrs. Harris, came to me after receiving a note from the principal's office. And then my parents weren't there anymore – just like that.

. . .

MOM AND DAD WERE DEAD. OUR HOUSE HAD BURNED TO THE ground. We had nothing apart from the clothes we had on and the things in our backpacks. Baldwyn, the oldest of us, was only nineteen at the time. He became both mother and father to us all. And nothing was ever the same again.

Being on the cusp of manhood, I knew one thing for sure — I needed to have all the fun I could before whoever was in charge of our lives and our deaths decided my life had to end. Nothing lasted anyway, so I'd never really thought any of the relationships I had would ever go anywhere.

Maybe I was emotionally stunted from my past – hell if I knew. But I knew one thing for certain — I couldn't stop thinking about Ember and how her life had turned out.

Something inside of me kept dragging my mind back to that woman and her little girl. They needed me, and I knew that without any shred of a doubt.

Yes, Ember made good money. But it took way too much time from her daughter. The inexplicable hissy fit Ember had just had told me that she was one overworked and overtired lady who needed something more than her family could provide.

She needs a good man in her life, too.

Sure, I hadn't been a good man until that point, but that didn't mean that I couldn't become one. I had the basics down. A great job. Financial security. A stable home. All I had to do was become a one-woman man.

Why does that thought make chills shoot through me?

After a short knock, my office door opened, and there were Madison and Aliana. "We're back," my employee said.

Madison wasted no time running into the office – high on sugar, no doubt. "She makes the best ice cream I've ever tasted! It was so good and creamy and sweet! I can't believe you guys make your own ice cream here. This place is the best. I mean it! I love this place. I could just live here," her mouth ran a mile a minute. Then she looked around the room. "Where's Mom?"

"Probably in her suite." I gave Alaina a nod of thanks. "Thanks for showing her a good time."

"I had a good time, too. See ya around, Maddy." She left us, closing the door behind her.

"Maddy?" I asked as I hadn't heard her mother call her by any nickname.

She'd begun running back and forth in front of the window. "Yeah, my friends at school call me that. And my best friend in the whole wide world, Stevie, calls me Mad. She's so crazy. Her real name isn't Stevie — it's Stephanie. But she says she's not that girly and likes to be called Stevie. And she says that I'm kind of crazy, so she calls me Mad. Not because I'm angry, but because I am like a mad scientist. She's silly. But I love her so much."

She would miss everyone if they moved here.

Ember was right about that. Madison would have to leave everyone she knew and loved behind. I knew she wasn't ready for such a drastic change. "You seem like you've got some energy to burn. I'll walk you to your room so you and your mom can start your fun day. I'm sure she's got something good planned out for you."

Skipping in front of me, she led the way to the elevator. "I don't know what she's planned cause she didn't tell me. But I know that I want to do some fun stuff and nothing boring."

Ember had her work cut out for her — and I felt a bit responsible for that. *Okay, I'm completely responsible for that.* Madison pulled an extra keycard out of her pocket just as we got to the door. "Mom gave me one of these, but I don't know how to use it." She handed it to me, then stepped back and began turning around and around in circles. "I'm getting dizzy," she squealed with delight.

I knew Ember was going to want to kick my ass for all the sugar her kid had eaten. When I opened the door, I heard an odd muffled sound. Peeking inside, I saw Ember lying face down on the bed — she was obviously crying her heart out.

I can't let Madison see her mom like this.

I had no idea what the hell to do, but I did know that I needed to entertain Madison until Ember pulled herself together. The hissy fit had turned into a crying jag, which told me that she was dealing with some deep issues.

Closing the door quietly not to bother Ember at all, I grabbed Madison's hand, stopping her dizzying circles as I led her away from the door. "How about I take you swimming?"

"I'll have to get my bathing suit." She pulled at me to turn back.

"I'll take you to the gift shop and get you a new one. And some arm floats would probably be a good idea too." I wasn't about to go diving into the pool if she got into any trouble, so the floats were a must. "Do you have a way to call your mom?" From what I'd seen with all the people who came to our resort, I knew most kids — even some as young as Madison — had their own cell phones.

Pulling a little one out of her back pocket, she nodded. "Yeah, I got a phone. I'll call her."

"No." I couldn't let her do that – Ember clearly needed some time to herself. Wiggling my fingers, I said, "Let me text her to tell her where I'm taking you. That way, she can come and find us when she's done with whatever she's doing."

"K." She handed me the phone then took advantage of being free, taking off like a streak of lightning to beat me to the elevator. "I'm gonna beat you, Cohen!"

"Yes, you are." I wasn't about to start running down the hall. I texted Ember the plan about taking her daughter swimming then waited to see if she'd reply.

No message arrived for a long time. And then, just as we stepped off the elevator and into the lobby, she texted back, *"Thank you."*

Wow, would you look at that?

A simple thanks. Not some convoluted crap for once.

Maybe all that crying has brought the girl I used to know back to the surface.

Ember was as cool as a cucumber back then. Level-headed, to be sure, but also as cool as shit. I could talk to her in a way that I couldn't talk to anyone else.

She was so different now. So worried about everything.

Maybe being a parent did that to people. How was I to know?

But I knew that the woman I'd fallen for was still inside that hot body. It's like I could see glimpses of her but couldn't bring her into focus. The real Ember, the one who could make me laugh, make me feel things no one else could, make me feel like I was someone special, was still there — somewhere. I just had to find her again.

In no time, Madison and I were at the indoor pool, and she was quick to start playing a game of Marco Polo with some other kids around her age.

She's a little social butterfly.

It was as if the kid couldn't meet a stranger. She liked everyone the very instant she met them. As I watched her playing and swimming around, I thought about how similar I was to this little girl.

When I met someone new, I treated them like a friend. And I'd keep treating them that way until they gave me a reason to stop. And if they did more than a few things that turned me off, I'd simply stop being around them.

That may have seemed shallow to some people. I'd been told by many of the women I'd stopped seeing that I was shallow and needed to learn that people had disagreements and arguments were a fact of life.

I knew disagreements and arguments had to happen at times. But I also knew that no one, male or female, needed to be shitty. I had no time for shitty people in my life.

I only allowed genuine people in my inner circle. And that meant my inner circle was on the small side. There were my brothers, of course. And their wives and kids – that was a given. I had two guy friends with whom I really enjoyed spending time. And so far, the only girl who'd made me want to spend all my time with her was Ember Wilson.

And she'd dumped me. Pretty shitty.

I shook off the negative thought about a person who had been mostly positive in my life; I knew she'd had valid reasons for ending things. At least they were valid in her mind. Mine? Not so much.

With six months passing between me dating Ashe and seeing Ember, I'd thought that to be plenty of time for Ashe to get the hell over herself. Besides, Ashe and I hadn't even dated for that long. Ember had not agreed.

"Can I jump off the diving board, Cohen?" Madison shouted out to me as she swam toward the deep end.

"No," I shouted right back. "And swim your little back-end right back to the shallow end, young lady."

Wearing a frown, she did as I said, and that's when I felt a hand on my shoulder. "Hey."

I found Ember there, a slight smile on her freshly washed face and her hair pulled back into a ponytail. Then she took a seat next to me. She sat so close that our legs touched, sending sparks of excitement and hope through me. "Feeling better?"

"Yeah. I know you saw me in the room. And I know I was wrong for saying what I said before storming out of your office like a lunatic. It's me — not you. Not you at all."

I felt a slow smile spreading across my face, feeling that today would be a good day after all.

CHAPTER 12
EMBER

I'd sat too close to him on the bench he'd been sitting on at the pool's edge. Our outer thighs touched — the contact was a bit too much for me, so I slid over a little to put some space between us.

With his eyes on the gap I'd created between us, he asked, "Do I make you feel uncomfortable?"

"Yes, you do." I laughed to lighten the blow. "You make me feel things I haven't felt in a long time."

"Things you haven't felt in, say, seven years?" His eyes moved up my body, lingering on my breasts before resting on my eyes.

"Yeah." I felt the heat of a blush on my cheeks, which ignited a smile from him. "Stop it."

"No." Placing his palm on the bench between us, he made sure the tips of his fingers touched my leg. "I adore the way you react to me. And I love the way I react to you."

More heat filled me, this time making my entire body hot. "Cohen, you need to stop. I came down here to apologize for how I acted. I did not come down here to accept your offer."

"So, you'll be leaving tomorrow then." His fingers fluttered against my leg as he tried to entice me into changing my mind.

"We've got tonight. Why not see what's left from seven years ago?"

"I've got my kid." Even as I said it, my body and soul wanted him, and I leaned against him as I whispered, "If not for her, I'd take you up on the one-night thing."

His voice went deep and sultry, "Come back alone then."

As a mother, he'd offended me, so I moved back away from him. "Just when I think you're great with kids, you go and say something like that."

"Why would you think that *I'm* great with kids?"

"By the way you've been with Madison – treating her nice but being stern and telling her to get back to the shallow end of the pool. And by taking her to swim just to give me time to get a hold of myself."

When I'd heard her ask him if she could jump off the diving board as she headed to the deep end, I was about to call out to her that she most certainly could not do that. But Cohen took care of it — and he'd done so in a way that I felt was rather spectacular for a man with no kids.

"Maybe watching my older brothers with their kids has rubbed off on me. If you want to know the truth, I felt guilty for letting Madison eat sugary stuff this morning. She came back riding a sugar high like I've never seen before. I figured that she needed to move that little body of hers to burn that shit off, or she'd end up a crying mess. Which makes me wonder… have you eaten a lot of sugar this morning?"

"No." I punched him in the arm. "Goof."

"Ah, so your mood comes from something other than food."

Nodding as if he'd solved the mystery of why I'd gone mental, he added, "Women cry about way too many things. I'm glad I'm not one. With the pressure of society to be all things to all people, and the hormones, plus the constant way a mother puts her kids — and family, for that matter — before herself, I don't envy you women. Not even a little. I'm glad I'm a man."

"That makes two of us," I joked.

"Glad to hear that." He leaned in close. "I like being a man with you too," he whispered.

With him so close, his hot breath flowing past my ear, I melted inside. My words came out shaky, "You're so bad."

He leaned back to put space between us again. "You know, if you wanted, I could have someone go to your suite and sit with Madison after she goes to sleep tonight. And then you could come to my office, and we could…"

"Cohen," I cautioned him. "I can't."

Shaking his head, he hissed, "Still not on birth control?"

"I'm not on anything. Not that that's the reason I'm saying no."

"Oh, now I get it." His eyes danced as he teased me, "It's been a while since you've done any…*grooming*. Not to worry — I couldn't care less about that."

"That's not it either." But he wasn't wrong. He'd been my last sexual encounter, so I hadn't done much grooming to my private regions since I had no idea when sex would be on the table for me again. "Let's talk about something — anything — else. Please."

"Good idea." He jerked his head to gesture to Madison, who was playing with some other kids. "Check out Miss Madison over there, making new friends."

"Yeah, so?" I had no idea what he was getting at.

"You might like to know that she told me she wished she could live here at the resort because she loves it so much. And then she hopped into that pool and joined those kids without any hesitation whatsoever. If you ask me, I think she would adjust to life here in no time."

"Didn't I say that we could talk about *anything* else?" I found that to have been rather stupid of me.

"You did," he went on with a knowing grin on his handsome face. "And I'm just pointing out how kids are so much better at adapting than adults are. And you know that I know a lot about having to adapt to situations that aren't nearly as nice as this one."

My heart immediately ached for him. He'd told me all about the house fire that had taken his parents when he was only eleven. We'd cried together over what he'd gone through when he was so young. And now I wanted to cry again.

His hand still splayed out between us. I laced my fingers through his. "You know a hell of a lot more about that than I do."

"*You* are the *only* woman I've ever trusted enough to tell that to. And the way you shared my pain was an amazing experience." His lips pulled to one side. "You know, I thought after we shared that, it meant you and me would be together forever. I gave you more of myself than I have ever given to anyone. And I felt like you gave me more of yourself too."

"I did." I'd been unable to hold myself back with him. "And I don't regret one moment of the time we shared."

"But you do regret being with me," he pointed out. "Because you broke up with me."

"No, I don't regret being with you." I had other regrets. And I finally felt that he should know about them. Or at least some of them. "I regret that I did things that would hurt my sister. I regret that I let my attraction to you override my loyalty to her."

"You're mad at yourself, not me." Bending his fingers, he pulled my hand into his. "Don't be mad at yourself, Ember. I think we had something special. I think we had something not everyone finds. I think we still might."

He had no idea how much I agreed. My heart hung heavy in my chest, knowing that he'd always be off-limits. Even if my family were able to get over it, how could I be with him after keeping his daughter a secret, especially from him? He would hate me when he found out the truth.

The entire week that we'd been together had played over and over again in my mind from the moment I had realized that I'd missed two monthly visits from Aunt Ruby — aka, my period.

Cohen and I had used a condom every time we'd had sex, save that one time. But I'd used my legs to hang onto him, not wanting to let him go as I came undone in a way I hadn't before. And at that moment, our daughter was made. I was sure of that.

Feeling like it was entirely my fault, I'd decided the burden was mine to carry — mine alone. Well, not until after I had tracked him down and saw him with that other chic. But still, I did make the decision not long after that happened.

His tight grip on my hand pulled me out of my thoughts, and I looked at him. "I can take the blame, Cohen. I can take the blame for everything. I was the one who wasn't loyal to my sister — not you. I knew I shouldn't be with a man my sister had been with. It was never your fault — not about a damn thing."

His head cocked a little to one side as he looked away from me. "No," he said, shaking his head before looking back at me. "I am at fault for some things too. I shouldn't have moved on to someone else so quickly. And I should've come to you, called you, done something to try and get you back. I guess that being rejected — a thing I'd never had to deal with in my entire life — took its toll on me and my self-esteem. I didn't want to face you again, only for you to tell me once more that what we had was over. I never wanted to hear those words come out of your mouth again."

He shook his head as if he was trying to shake off the memories from the past. "Yet here we are. And, baby, let me tell you that I must've done some growing up because I'm prepared to hear those words come out of your mouth as many times as I have to. Wanna know why?"

Mesmerized by him, I asked, "Why is that, Cohen?"

"Because when you find the right one, you can take the pain." He pulled our clasped hands up and kissed mine. "You can take the pain of hearing words you never wanted to hear again because the pain is worth it if you can get the girl in the end."

I gulped back a knot that tried to form in my throat. "And if you don't get the girl in the end, then what?" I asked.

His broad chest rose as he took a deep breath while looking up at the ceiling. "Nah, I can't think that way." His eyes fell on mine. "Life is too short, Ember. You know what I'm saying."

"Cohen, you know that I can't hurt my sister or my parents."

"I'm offering you a job. That's all they have to know right now. I'm offering you a job that has so many perks that you'll hardly pay a thing out of your paycheck. Plus, you'll get to spend tons more time with your daughter. Only someone who is thinking only of themselves would tell you not to take it just because I'm the one offering it." Pressing his forehead against mine, he added, "Call Ashe and see what she has to say. That's all I'm asking. Make the call, Ember."

"What if she tells me that you're only offering me this so you can screw me?" I knew she'd say that too.

Ember's proficiency at finding the negative in any given situation was a gift — a horrible one — but a gift, nonetheless. "If she says that to you, you can let her know that it's not true."

"But you know it is. Well, sort of." A sexy smile curved her plump, completely kissable lips. "You do want to screw me. I know you do."

I leaned over, putting my lips right up to her ear. "I prefer calling it making love, baby," I whispered.

I felt the heat radiating off her skin as she pushed me back. Although she did it playfully, I knew she didn't want Madison to see us that close. "What did I tell you about calling me that?" she huffed as she waved her hand in front of her face to cool herself off. "God, Cohen." A deep breath settled her down as her face lost most of the red color my little whisper had caused. "You're so — so…"

"Amazing." I nodded. "Yes, I know."

"Shit, I forgot what we were even talking about." She smacked my upper thigh. "You're so bad."

Placing my hand on top of hers while keeping it on my leg, I grazed her knuckles with my thumb. "I'm gonna keep your hand right here. Just so you don't smack me again. K?"

She jerked her hand away. "No. It's definitely not okay." Her eyes moved to Madison, who was playing with the other kids and not noticing us at all.

"I could kiss you right now, and she wouldn't even notice."

The way her head snapped to look at me, her mouth agape, told me she wasn't into my great idea. "Don't you dare!"

With a chuckle, I watched her cheeks turn red again. "Making you blush is way too easy."

"I remember what we were talking about now," she quickly changed the subject. "If my sister says that you just want to hire me so you can screw me, then I should say something like... no, he's not?"

My eyes rolled all of their own accord. "Yeah, that's a brilliant argument that you've got there."

She crossed her arms over her chest. "What would you have me say, smartypants?"

"Well, if I were you, then I would say something like this, 'Ashe, you don't know Cohen anymore. He's grown up since you two messed around.' And that's true."

She held up one hand. "Hold it. I can't say that you two just messed around, or she'll get pissy. She considered you her boyfriend. So, change that."

"Fine." *Women! Geeze.* "What I'm getting at is that you need to say a lot of nice stuff about me. You know – like how I've grown out of my womanizing ways." I thought I'd let her know about my aversion to the word she used for me. "I prefer being called a womanizer to man-whore, by the way."

"Well, *excuse* me, sir." It was her turn to do an eye-roll. "Can I point out that you have most certainly not outgrown your womanizing ways?"

"No, you may not." I wasn't going to let her keep seeing me in that light. "You're not paying much attention to the things I've told you, Ember Wilson. I want *you*. Only *you*. And as long as I think I've got a shot in hell with you, then you will be the only woman on my radar."

"Yeah, that's not stalkerish at all, Cohen. Does this work with all the girls?" She laughed, but I knew she meant it.

"I wouldn't know, Ember. I've never said these things to anyone but you." I had no idea how she could be so blind. "I trust you. Even though you hurt me, I still trust you. I know you had your reasons for breaking things off with me, which I respect. Ember, I respect you in all ways. I don't just want to get into your pants. I want to spend time with you – getting to know you even better. I can't say that about any other woman."

Her eyes held mine as her lips parted slightly. "Cohen, that's the nicest thing anyone's ever said to me."

"I mean everything I say to you."

Nodding, she blinked rapidly as if she were afraid tears might escape. "I believe you. But that doesn't change a thing."

"Well, it should." *I wish it would change everything.*

Looking away, she ran the back of her hand over her eyes. "So, you think if I tell my sister and parents that you're a good man now, they'll be all for me taking Madison and moving away from them?"

"It's only a little over two and a half hours from here to there. You could visit every weekend if you wanted to. And they could come up here and see you as well. Hell, you know I'd put them up here at the resort for free, right?"

Her eyes lit up. "Hold on. That might work."

"You never thought about the fact that they could stay here for free when they came to see you?" I laughed. "Do I have to spell everything out for you, Ember? I want you here. I'd do anything to get you to stay. *Anything.*"

The light in her eyes went even brighter. "Anything?"

I wasn't sure I liked what I saw in them either. "Well, almost anything."

"Oh. Cause I was gonna say that if you want me to consider this, then you should stop pressuring me."

"If I stop pressuring you, then you'll stop thinking about it." I wasn't stupid. But I wasn't asking her much about her life either. And when a guy was completely into a girl, he asked about the girl's life. I had been paying attention to how my brothers had snagged their wives. "Let's change subjects here. Since you want less pressure."

"I'm game."

I caught some movement out of the corner of my eye as Madison once again made for the deep end. I stared right at her, my eyes narrowed, and she knew I'd caught her. She immediately turned around with an adorable impish grin on her face. "Oops, wrong way."

"If you think I'm not watching you, you're wrong, young lady." I pointed at her then back at my eyes. "Eagle eyes, right here."

Madison giggled all the way back to the other kids. "Okay, okay, okay. I won't try it again."

Ember's expression turned cloudy. "Wow, I didn't even notice her doing that."

I had the feeling she hadn't noticed because parenting had taken a backseat for a brief moment – that was good. She needed to think about herself for a second, about her future. And my role in it. "So, how're things with you, Ember? I mean, really. How are things going? I doubt you were upset by being offered a great job and a place to live too. There must be more that's bothering you."

She scrunched up her nose, and I could tell it was hard for her to talk about herself. "It's not easy, relying on my parents to help so much with Madison," she answered. "They're getting older, and they've got their own problems to deal with. Mom had to take Madison to Ashe's one day last week so she could take Dad to the doctor. He was having dizzy spells."

"Taking care of a kid — even one as good as Madison — can be strenuous. I'm sure they're doing the very best they can, but raising kids is a younger person's game. Don't you think?"

From what I'd seen from my brothers' families, it took a tremendous amount of effort to take care of kids.

"You think I don't feel guilty about what they're doing for me?" she snapped. "I never wanted to depend on them for a thing. This wasn't my dream. But things changed, and I went towards the direction I saw best. Staying on at the storage unit job was a dead-end. I started at a minimum wage, and in three years, my pay only increased by a lousy fifty cents. I couldn't afford to live on my own — I had to stay in my childhood bedroom with my kid. It was humiliating. I had to do something. And I know it might seem sort of drastic, but I couldn't take it anymore. I couldn't take facing the people I'd grown up with looking at me like I was some sad loser. So, when I saw the oilfield job in the paper, I went for it."

"You took that giant leap. You can take another one. One that will change things for the better. You'll have plenty of money, plenty of opportunities to advance your career. You'll have plenty of spare time."

Still, she shook her head. "And you're not going to let this go, are you?"

Should I let this go? Should I just walk away and leave her alone?

"Ember, I think you've been thinking about your daughter for so long that you can't even think about what might be good for you." I couldn't just walk away from her. "I bet there's a part of you that thinks your parents are better at raising your daughter than you."

The way her chest caved in as she exhaled told me I'd hit the nail on the head. "Cohen, I was twenty-one when I gave birth to Madison. Even though plenty of women have kids much younger than that, I felt like a complete amateur. I'd never even babysat kids before. And I'd never held a newborn. Madison felt so fragile in my arms every time I held her. I felt that she was safer in my mother's arms than she was in mine."

Draping my arm around her shoulders, my heart ached for

her. "Oh, baby. I'm so sorry you had to go through that. I can't imagine how awful you must've felt."

"Cohen, thanks for the hug, but please stop. I don't want Madison to see." She shrugged her shoulders as I moved my arm. "Thanks."

"Sure." *She won't even let me hug her. I bet she won't let anyone hug her.* "Did you receive a lot of emotional support from your parents, as well as their physical support?"

"Sort of. They did the best they could. Mom had her hands full with the baby in the first few months." Sniffling, she ran the back of her hand across her eyes. "I finally caught up around the third month. Madison had gained weight, of course, so she didn't feel quite as breakable as she had in the beginning. But I did find that Mom didn't step back as much as I would've wanted her to."

"So, you felt like she'd taken over mothering your baby." I couldn't imagine what that must've felt like. "And you didn't feel like you could say anything to your mom about that?"

"I said a little — here and there. Not much, though. I felt so much guilt about bringing them that burden that I didn't want to come off as ungrateful." She wiped her eyes again. "God, Cohen. This isn't really the time or place to talk about this."

"You're right. You two should come to my place. Maybe you could spend the night there. And I'm not asking you just so I can get into your pants, so don't even go there. I just think that you could use a friend to talk to. I bet you haven't talked to anyone about all of this."

"And sound like an ungrateful jackass?" She shook her head. "No, I haven't talked to anyone about this. I don't know what it is about you, but I lose control of my mouth whenever I'm with you."

I saw her blush when she realized the innuendo in her words but decided I'd give her a pass – this time. "That's because we're good for each other. Mine does the same, but only when I'm with you." There was so much she needed to talk about — needed to get out.

"Yeah, I remember how easy it was for us to talk to each other — even though it was only for a week."

"I grew more with you in that week than I had before and since. There's just something about being with the right person that makes things grow."

Her lips formed a thin line, making her look a little unsure. "Cohen, there's so much more now than there was back then. It seems insurmountable to me. I'm sorry."

I didn't want to hear that shit. "Hey, what about the father? Why didn't you tell him about the pregnancy or let him know he had a kid? He could've shared some responsibilities after the baby was born."

Water splashed as Madison swam up to the side of the pool. "My tummy hurts, Momma. Can you get me out and take me to the room?"

"Sure, sweetie. Gotta go, Cohen." She rushed to the side of the pool, lifting Madison out. In seconds, they were walking away.

CHAPTER 14
EMBER

Saved by the bell!

Thanks to Madison's tummy troubles, I'd escaped the dreaded question Cohen had asked me about her father. "That ice cream has gotten to you, huh?"

"Yeah. I'll be okay once I go potty." She held my hand, looking up at me. "I'm glad you came to the pool to watch me, Momma."

Just as I reached out to open the door to leave the pool area, a hand came from behind me, beating me to it. "Allow me, ladies." It seemed that Cohen had caught up to us. His body behind mine made my knees turn weak, especially when he made sure to graze me a bit.

"Thanks," Madison said. "And thanks for watching me while I swam. Sorry about trying to go to the deep end, Cohen."

"I get it," he said as he walked alongside me. "Kids gotta test their limits. I've noticed that with my brothers' kids anyway. I'm not exactly a pro at knowing things about kids."

"Well, I think you're great." Madison looked around me to give him her biggest smile.

He smiled right back at her. "I think you're great too, Maddy."

"Maddy?" I had to ask.

"Yeah, my friends call me that, Mom."

"And as your friend, Maddy, I'd like to invite you and your mother out to lunch. You remember the pizza place I told you about, right?"

"Mom! Please! Please! I'll do anything!"

"I thought your stomach hurt," I reminded her, as she seemed to have forgotten.

"Mom, please don't talk about that right now. I'll be better soon. So, can we go?"

Cohen bumped his shoulder against mine. "Come on, Ember. How can it hurt?"

It can hurt my ability to keep certain secrets from you.

"Oh, alright." I had to give in — for my kid's sake.

At least that's what I'm telling myself.

"Cool, I'll be in my office whenever you girls are ready to go." He pushed the button for the elevator. "I'm gonna go check on some things. See you soon."

Madison and I got onto the elevator, and I found my daughter beaming at Cohen as the doors closed. "I'm glad you sat and talked to Cohen, Mom. He's nice."

"Yeah, he's nice." If things had been different, then I would've fallen right back into the man's extremely capable arms. But things weren't different.

As soon as we got to our room, Madison ran to the bathroom. I went to sit on the small sofa and picked up the television remote. My mind was on all the things Cohen and I had talked about and all the things he'd offered me and Madison.

And he did all that without knowing that Madison was his daughter.

My heart felt as if it were smiling at the fact that Cohen just wanted me around because he genuinely liked and cared about me. It didn't have a thing to do with any responsibility or obligation he felt towards me or our daughter. And that felt amazing.

"Momma, I'm done."

Getting up, I went to tend to her. "I'm coming."

She'd stripped down to nothing. "I'm gonna take a bath, and I need you to wash my hair. And I want you to blow dry it, and after that, can you use your hair straightener to make it look pretty and shiny?"

"That's a bit too much for a trip to a pizza joint." I turned on the bathwater for her. "But I'll wash your hair and dry it. Then I think a ponytail will do just fine."

With one hand on her hip, she looked at me like I had lost my mind. "Mom! We're going out with Cohen, and we both need to look nice."

For a second, I felt as if the tables had turned, and my kid was the parent, not me. But then that stopped, and I said, "We're not *going out* with Cohen. We're going to meet him to get something to eat and play some games. I'm taking my car. We're not even going to ride with him. This isn't a date, so don't make it sound that way." The last thing I needed was for her to go back talking about how we went out on a date with Cohen Nash.

"Can you just do my hair the way I asked you to?" She climbed into the bathtub then handed me the small bottle of shampoo provided by the resort. "Use this one instead of the stuff you brought from home. It smells better."

I had no idea how bougie my kid had become. "Since when do you care what your hair smells like?" I put a small amount of shampoo into my palm then sniffed it. *Oh, that is nice.*

"Since always, Mom. Come on, rub it in and let it set, so the smell gets all up in there." She turned her back to me, sitting cross-legged in the tub. "After I get out, you should get in and take a shower and wash your hair with this stuff, so you'll smell as good as I'm gonna."

Finally, I understood where she'd learned this from. "Your Aunt Ashe has some explaining to do."

"Why?" She laughed. "Oh, cause she's the one who fixes me up. She likes to play with my hair. She says it's so much thicker than yours and hers. And she told me that it looks better when it's straightened than when it's just left free. There are too many crazy waves when you don't do anything to it."

Just like your father's wavy hair.

If Cohen hadn't worn his hair short now, and the waves hung to his shoulders the way they'd done back then, I had a sneaky suspicion that Madison would've pointed out how alike their hair looked.

Thank God he cut it!

"I took a shower this morning — before you woke up. I'm not about to take another one just to go eat some pizza." Massaging the shampoo into her thick hair, I found I was enjoying myself. "I guess it's the scent of the shampoo, but I don't want to rush this the way I usually do."

"Yeah, good smells make me happy too." She let out a sigh. "I love it here, Momma. I wish we never had to leave."

We don't.

Well, if I took Cohen's offer, we wouldn't have to leave. But I couldn't take his offer no matter how generous it was. My family meant more to me than that.

I knew Mom and Dad had their hands full with Madison. But I also knew they wouldn't change a thing if they had the choice. They loved her as if she were their own. And she loved them too. "Wouldn't you miss your grandparents if we never left this place?"

"They could come too. But only sometimes cause Gramps has all those doctor's appointments."

"Well, when they couldn't be here, wouldn't you miss them?" I was sure she'd miss them. She'd hadn't gone more than a few days without seeing them since the day she was born.

Turning to face me, she had the oddest expression. "Mom, why do you keep saying that?"

"Lean back and let me rinse your hair." I didn't know what to tell her. I couldn't say that we could stay if we wanted. I couldn't tell her that because she would absolutely want to stay.

"Okay." She leaned back, closing her eyes tightly. "Try not to get any soap in my eyes, Mom."

"I'll try. You keep them closed real tight now." Using a disposable cup that was already in the bathroom, I filled it with water from the tap then poured it over her soapy hair until the water ran clear. "There we go. You're all done now."

"Great!" She jumped up and grabbed a towel off the towel rack. "If you won't take a shower, at least change your clothes."

Standing up, I noticed that I'd gotten a fair amount of water on me while I was washing and rinsing her hair. "Ugh."

With the towel wrapped around her, she ran out of the bathroom and into the room. I followed along, not quite in the rush she apparently was in.

Opening the closet, she looked at the clothes hanging there. "You didn't bring me any more nice dresses?" She looked at me over her shoulder with narrowed eyes. "Gee wiz, Mom. I can't wear the one I wore yesterday. Ugh."

"Sorry." I took a seat on the sofa again.

"You could take me down to the store that Cohen took me to and got me that bathing suit. There were lots of pretty dresses down there."

"And I bet they're a pretty penny too. Just find something in the closet, you little princess." I wasn't about to go drop a hundred bucks on a dress from a resort shop. I wasn't a fool with money after all. "When we get back home, I've gotta get you some new tennis shoes for school. I can't be wasting money, you know."

If I took the job Cohen offered me, money would no longer be an issue.

Hell, if I tell Cohen that Madison is his kid, then she'd have everything she could ever want.

Am I shortchanging my own daughter just to avoid upsetting my family?

That was the first time I'd thought about things in that light. I hadn't known that Cohen had made himself into a rich man. And I had thought that he was still living the same lifestyle that he used to. It seemed that he might not be if he wanted the two of us to be a thing.

This older Cohen Nash was a little different than how I'd imagined him.

Maybe I'm shortchanging myself and my kid. And Cohen, too.

"Mom," she shouted at me. "You're just sitting there. Come on. We need to get ready. And you need to change, fix your hair, put on some makeup, and you need to help me get ready too!"

"Madison, there's no reason to get all gussied up. Cohen doesn't care about stuff like that." I got up to find something to wear since I'd gotten my clothes wet. "Some jeans and a t-shirt are good enough."

With her mouth hanging open, she looked at me with wide eyes. "Mom — have you even looked at him? He's so handsome. And he dresses nice too. Can't you see that he likes you?"

A jolt of laughter erupted from my mouth. "What?" She couldn't say that around our family. "He does not. You need to find your filter, my girl."

"Why don't you like him?" She finally picked out a shirt and some jeans to put on and carried them to the bed.

"He was your *aunt's* boyfriend. How come you can't seem to remember that?" I went to the closet to find something to put on, knowing that if I didn't hurry, she'd just keep bugging me.

"I don't know why you think Aunt Ashe will care if he and you become boyfriend and girlfriend. She's got Uncle Mike. And it was a long, long time ago when he was her boyfriend anyway. I don't think she'll care at all."

"I think you're wrong." I picked out a pink t-shirt and some faded jeans. "What about this?"

She looked at it with horror in her eyes. "No way! Wear some jeans that aren't faded, at least."

Putting back the faded pair, I pulled out the newest pair I possessed. My daughter was right. They looked much better.

I could help wondering if that was the only thing she was right about.

CHAPTER 15

COHEN

Tossing a skeeball up the long ramp, I made it right into the middle hole. "Thirty points!"

"Lucky," Madison said as she tossed hers, getting it into the ten-point hole.

"Way to go!" I gave her a high-five as the tickets we'd won poured out of our machines. "We're gonna get tons of prizes."

"We sure are." She looked around to find what she wanted to play next. "Mom's waving at us. The pizza's on the table. We better go eat."

She took off, running like a cat through a jungle, dodging other kids and adults with no effort whatsoever. I watched Ember as she placed slices of pizza on plates for us. A pitcher of beer sat on the table too — which I found promising.

Maybe she's ready to chill out and accept the inevitable.

Ember had picked out a booth for us to sit in, and Madison slid into the seat across from her. The way she sat right at the edge of her seat made it impossible for me to take the seat next to hers. So, I had to sit next to her mother, who scooted over for me to sit down. "Want a beer?"

"Yep." A steaming slice of cheese pizza sat on the plate in front of me. "Yummy — my favorite."

"Mine too!" Madison bit into her slice. "Mmmm, this is so good."

Ember filled two mugs with beer and passed one to me. "She'll only eat cheese pizza. That's why I ordered it. You can't get pizza by the slice here. It's a whole pie or nothing."

"I really do like cheese pizza, Ember." I wasn't lying.

Her brows shot up. "You do?"

"Yeah, I do." I took a bite to show her how much I liked it. "Yum."

"K, then." Laughing a little, she took a drink of her beer. "The waitress said there's gonna be a dance-off in a little bit. The winner gets five thousand tickets."

Madison wiggled around, dancing in her seat. "I'm in!" She looked at me. "What about you, Cohen? You wanna dance too?"

Ember saved me, putting her hand on my shoulder. "Sorry, sweetie. Kids only."

"Oh. Well, I guess that's good. Fewer people dancing that way." She took another bite of the pizza as she looked around – sizing up the competition, no doubt.

Madison took a few more bites then put the outer rim of the crust on her plate.

Just like I do.

I placed my uneaten crust on my plate and noticed the way Madison looked at it. Ember put another piece in its place. "Here you go." She looked at Madison. "You want another piece too?"

"No thanks." She sat back, taking her attention off my plate. "I wonder when the dance thingy is gonna start."

"Drink your milk while you're waiting," Ember urged her. "You want strong teeth and bones, don't you?"

Madison picked up the cup and gulped all the milk down before putting her cup back on the table. "Finished."

"And in record time, too," Ember congratulated her.

Music filled the air as someone said over the speaker

system, "Can I get all the boys and girls to come to the main stage for a dance-off, please?"

Madison was gone before I could even tell her to break a leg. "Wow, she's fast."

"She certainly is." Ember took a drink as she eyed me over the rim.

"You're looking a lot more relaxed."

She put the mug down. "Yeah, I'm feeling that way."

"Have you thought about coming to my place to spend the night?"

"No." She pointed to the empty side of the table. "Think you might want to sit over there now?"

"No." I wasn't moving. I liked being this close to her. "I like the way your energy feels, and I'm gonna stick close to it."

"Okay then." Moving around, she put one leg under her, moving sideways in the booth so she could face me. "So, I told you how *my* life has been going. Now it's your turn to tell me how *yours* has been going. Like how you ended up owning a resort."

"Well, we have some cousins who we never knew about. They inherited a ranch in Carthage, Texas, from a grandfather they never met. We're related through their mother's side of the family. It was their grandfather on their father's side who left them everything. And everything included billions of dollars."

"No shit?"

"No shit." Wrapping my hand around the cold mug, I pulled it closer to me. "They grew up really poor, despite their grandfather being wealthy. Their father chose love over money — leaving his inheritance behind. So, they got it and wanted to help some of their family members climb the ladder too. And that's how my brothers and I got the money to build the resort. It took lots of hard work and long hours to put things together, but we did it. And now we're all doing rather well."

"So, you've been too busy to do much of your womanizing

these last few years then, huh?" She pulled the glass to her lips as she waited for my answer.

"I have been pretty busy."

"Am I to believe that you've been as busy as I have?"

"You know that's like comparing apples to oranges. You had a kid to take care of while I was still footloose and fancy-free." I didn't want to compare what I'd done to what she'd done. Her job must have been so much harder than mine.

Nodding, she finished off the remainder of the beer in her mug then refilled it. "Must've been nice."

"You must've had some free time too, Ember."

"Yeah, I've had free time." She clung to the full mug as if it might help her in some way. "But when I get free time, I mostly catch up on my sleep."

I wasn't sure what to think. She'd told me that her mother had pretty much taken over taking care of Madison. But then, at other times, she talked like she was always busy with her kid. "So, which is it, Ember? Your mom takes care of her, or you do?"

Narrow eyes scanned me. "What do you mean?"

"I mean that you've said things that made me think your mom has taken primary care of Madison. And you've also said how you've taken primary care of her. I'm not trying to argue with you, but it can't be both, right?"

"Like you know what it's like to raise a child." She huffed. "Mom and Dad have taken the place of a father. I still do all the things a mother would do. Plus, I go to work to provide for her. And I do that all on my own. So, for your information, even with my family's help, my life is still full of raising Madison."

"Okay." I hadn't meant to rile her up. "I was just asking. You're right – I don't have a clue what raising a kid is like. I thought we could talk about anything. But it seems I was wrong."

"When you accuse me of lying, it makes having a normal conversation hard." She took a long drink.

"I didn't accuse you of lying. I just said that you've said some things that are sort of conflicting, is all. And now that you've clarified things, I get it. I do know that both parents work ridiculously hard to take care of their kids. So, thank you for clearing things up for me."

"You're welcome." She put the mug down then pushed it away from her — which I thought to be a good idea since she was already on the moody side. "I don't mean to be a jackass. It's just not easy to explain how hard it is to raise a kid to someone who doesn't know. But there are upsides, too. Getting to watch her smile for the first time was great. Getting to watch her take her first steps was amazing. And watching her as she drifts off to sleep makes my heart sing."

Suddenly, she furrowed her brows as if she had remembered some unpleasant thought in the middle of all those happy memories.

"I bet it does." Madison was one adorable kid, and she had her mother's doe-like eyes, too. "How does it feel to look at another human being and see yourself in her?"

I was hoping the question would clear up whatever had put the frown on her face, but it only seemed to make it worse. Her head dropped. and she closed her eyes. "I need to eat." She got a piece of pizza and took a bite without answering my question.

"This is the first time you've eaten today, isn't it?" I twirled my finger through her ponytail as she ate.

"Yeah." She took another bite.

"Being around me has affected you in both good and bad ways, huh?"

Nodding, she took another bite.

At least she's honest.

"You know, I've never even thought about having kids. I

know I don't like crying kids. How'd you handle all the crying when she was a baby?"

"Like any mother handles it, I guess. I wouldn't say I liked it, but I knew that if she was crying, it meant she needed something. I would check her diaper to see if it needed changing. And if that weren't it, then I'd make her a bottle to see if she was hungry. And sometimes I couldn't figure out what the cause was, and I would just hold her and rock her and try not to cry myself."

"God, that sounds horrible."

"Sometimes it was horrible," a smile came over her pink lips, even as she said the words. "I will never forget the first time she pooped and had a blowout in her diaper. Stinky, mushy poop went all the way up her back. I had to throw away the onesie she'd had on because it was completely ruined. And I had to give her a bath, which made her mad, and she cried the entire time. She was about three months old at the time. I'd just begun trying to figure out how to take care of her, and then she went and did that to me."

"Where was your mom when all this crap happened?"

"She was there. Coaching me — laughing hysterically. I didn't find it funny at the time. But later, I did. Much later — much, much later."

"So, you had Madison before your sister had any babies of her own, didn't you?" I wondered how that had gone over.

"Yeah. She'd moved out by the time I had Madison. She and this girl shared an apartment. But she was still there for me a lot. And she made sure to spend time with Madison at least once a week. She always brought her pretty little dresses and would dress her up while chastising me for only dressing her onesies all the time."

"You've never been into fashion," I pointed out. "I liked that about you. You weren't worried about all the stupid shit that so many other Southern Belles worried about. Perfect nails. Perfect eyebrows."

She ran her hand over her brows. "Are mine too full?"

"They're perfect." I had to laugh. "Well, maybe I'm wrong. Maybe you are into at least one perfect thing."

"I mean, I like to look presentable. But I'm not about to spend a fortune on myself when I've got a kid to provide for. As a matter of fact, the last thing I bought myself was a couple of pairs of blue jeans on sale." Her eyes searched the dancers on stage, looking for Madison. "It makes me way happier to buy things for my daughter other than for myself."

"Spoken like a true mom." But that was precisely why she needed a man in her life. She wouldn't *need* to buy things for herself if she had a man to spoil her.

I'd buy her everything she could ever want.

"Quite a few kids have given up and fallen out of the competition up there." I waved at Madison when I saw her looking my way. "Keep it up, tiny dancer!"

"Damn, that girl's got some moves, doesn't she?" Cohen pointed out.

"She's been in dance class since she was three. Ashe made sure of that." Again, I was reminded how much my sister had done for my kid. I owed Ashe my loyalty for all she'd done for Madison and me.

"Your sister did love to dance." His head dropped. "Sorry. Bet you didn't wanna hear me say that. I don't think sometimes."

"I'm not like that, and you know it." Sliding my hand along his shoulder, I rode the wave of excitement that touching him took me on. "You were with her first. You were with her longer. I'm the interloper — not her."

Turning his head to look at me, his eyes appeared softer than usual. "Ember, I may have spent more time with her than I did with you, but you're the one — you're the only one — who has ever gotten into my heart."

His eyes can't lie.

If there was a way in hell that I could have him without hurting my family, I would make it happen. But I couldn't see how I could manage the task without letting everyone know that I was a betraying liar. A long as a shit liar, too. Seven years, I'd lied. Seven long years.

And it was time to add Cohen to the list of people I'd lied to. And that wasn't easy either. It had been so easy to tell myself that he was living a life that had no room for Madison in it, that I wasn't depriving him of anything. But now, seeing him interact with her, hearing about his life, I wasn't so sure.

"You're the only one who's gotten into my heart too." Lying to someone who I had been so close to falling in love with proved to be maddening.

If I could trust that Cohen finding out about being Madison's father wouldn't lead to my family finding out about my secret, then I would've told him. But I knew that wasn't possible.

Not that he'd go to Houston to tell them to their faces, but he'd undoubtedly tell his brothers, who would tell others, and eventually, it would trickle down to my family's ears.

It had been ages since I'd been so angry at myself over what I'd done. Having Cohen right there, knowing I was being deceitful and doing things, once again, that went against my moral character, made me so pissed off at myself that I could barely contain it.

I poured myself another beer to lessen the fury that had built inside of me. Cohen watched me as I took a long drink. "You know, I can take you and Madison back to the resort or to my place, whichever you want. You can just leave your car here, and I'll have someone from the resort pick it up for you."

Does he think I'm getting drunk?

"That's okay. We won't be going to your place, so that's not an issue. And I'm fine to drive back to the resort." I looked at the beer, of which I'd already downed a quarter. "I know I'm consuming more than average, but I'll stop right now if you think I'm getting tipsy."

"It's just that I see no reason for you to drive after drinking. I weigh more than you, and I've only drunk about half a beer, so it hasn't affected me. I don't mind at all. I can drive you guys back to the resort." He smiled to lessen the blow. "You know, that way, you can drink as much as you want."

"I'm not a lush, Cohen." I pushed the mug away from me. "It's just that I'm on edge with you. I hardly ever drink anyway — maybe a few times a year on special occasions."

"Even more of a reason for me to drive. Come on, Ember, it's not a big deal. No more arguing. I'm going to text my assistant and have her come get your car and take it back for you."

"No." I wasn't going to let him take over. "I'm fine. And we're not leaving here for at least another hour. It's not up to you, anyway." I'd gotten myself worked up. "Can you let me out so I can go to the bathroom?"

He got up, but as I moved past him, he caught me by the arm. "You don't have to be so damn prickly, Ember. I don't know why you're getting yourself so worked up."

Closing my eyes, I knew I wasn't acting like myself. "Cohen, I'm sorry. I'll get myself in check. Just let me go."

"You're making yourself crazy, and I think I know why." He pulled me closer to him. "You don't have to keep fighting yourself about me. Your family *will* accept things — eventually. Trust me on this. You don't have to do this to yourself. You don't have to do this to *us*. You do realize what you're doing is hurting me too, right?"

Fuck yes, I do!

"I've gotta go to the bathroom. Let me go. Please." I couldn't talk to him about the pain I was causing him. If he ever found out what I'd done, he'd surely hate me.

"Think about what I've said. Please." He let me go, and I took off to get to the bathroom before I started crying in front of the whole place.

Luckily, there was no one else in the bathroom as I went straight to the sink and splashed my face with cold water. I had to stop this. I couldn't be with Cohen. I couldn't pretend I hadn't lied for seven fucking years.

Somehow, I had to get away from him and stay away from him. We only had one more night at the resort. If I were here alone, I would've left already. But Madison would have a fit if we left early.

Looking at myself in the mirror, I tried to figure out what I could do to stop being mad at myself — at least until I was far away from Cohen.

I had a job I had to get to after I dropped Madison off with my parents the next day anyway. I could kick the shit out of myself while I was alone at work. Until then, I had to stop doing it. I had to fool myself into thinking that I hadn't gone against my morals for such a long time. I had to fool myself into thinking that I was a good person.

Apparently, I'd been able to fool myself about that for a long time. But being around Cohen brought out the truth. Somehow, being around him made me face the kind of person I really was.

I am a liar.

I supposed that lying to my family hadn't felt so bad since I wasn't really hurting them by doing it. But lying to Cohen and Madison was different. I was hurting them both by keeping the truth to myself.

"You have to tell everyone the truth, Ember Wilson." I stared myself down in the mirror, trying to intimidate that liar inside of me.

It's been seven years! No one will ever believe a word I say from now on if I come clean.

I tried not to think about it. I just had to shut things down in my mind to get through the rest of the day. I could leave early in the morning. Madison always understood when I had to go to work. I would tell her that we had to get back to Houston early enough so I could get packed up and take off for work.

Taking deep breaths, I finally got myself under control, enough to go back out and face the man I'd had a baby with but had kept it a secret from the entire world.

"Mom!" came Madison's voice just as I walked out of the bathroom. "There you are." She shook a handful of tickets at me. "I didn't win, but I came second place, and I got a thousand tickets!"

"That's great, sweetie!" I caught someone moving in my peripheral vision and turned to find Cohen standing there.

"I don't see how that other kid beat her," he said as he patted her on top of the head. "She danced her butt off."

"He was a good dancer, though," she admitted. "Better than me. For now, anyway. I'm gonna get better for the next time we come back here. And I'll win then."

There will never be a next time.

Cohen was quick to pick up where she left off. "We should schedule your next visit. I'm going to comp it. When will you have some time off again, Ember?"

"Oh, I don't know. And I can't let you give us a free room, Cohen." I couldn't ever return. Being around him was turning me into a crazy person.

"It's not a problem." He took the tickets that Madison was shaking at him before she ran off to play more games. "I can't simply let you go without knowing when I'll see you again."

You have to let me go.

"My job doesn't work that way. I never know when I'm going to have time off. We'll just have to play it by ear. But I don't want you to think I'll be coming back anytime soon." *Or ever.*

"You know that I can come to you, right?" He took my hand, leading me back to the table. "I don't expect you to always come here. Anywhere you are, I can go. Surely you can leave the oil rig when your partner is working. I can get us a room or rent a B&B or something."

"Cohen, I don't know." But I did. I knew I couldn't do anything else with him after I left the next morning. "First of all, I haven't agreed to see you. So, there's that."

"I know I might sound kind of desperate." He slid into the booth behind me, trapping me. "You're leaving tomorrow. And I've got this feeling that you're going to try to forget about me. Ember, I don't want to lose you again. I didn't fight for you last time, but I will this time. You and I have something. You know that."

He was saying all the right things. Resisting him would be so much easier if he weren't so damn perfect.

"Well, for now, let's just chill out on the whole seeing each other thing. I've got lots to think about, you know. My family and my kid." Sharp pains shot through my stomach as my body fought me on everything I said. *She's his kid too!*

It seemed that my conscience had gone to war with the immoral part of me. I was left volleying back and forth to see which one would miss the ball and who would end up winning the game.

"I'm not okay with that. Your kid adores me, and I adore her. So, you can't use her as an excuse. And we've already discussed the fact that anyone who wouldn't want to see you spending more time with your daughter doesn't have your best interests at heart anyway." His fingers moved slowly along my jawline before resting his hand on the back of my neck. He used to do that all the time, right before he'd kiss me.

"Please, don't." I couldn't take a kiss from him. It would break me — I was sure of it.

"If you're worried about Madison seeing us, don't be. I can see her from here, and she has her back turned to us since she's playing a game. I think you need a reminder of how good we are together."

"No." I moved his hand off me. "I'm not going to let you charm me into this again. You know why, and I'm tired of explaining it only for you to act as if none of it matters. It matters to me. And that's all you need to know." I put both hands on his broad chest. "Let me out. We're leaving. I'm done arguing with you over this."

"Ember, wait." He stayed put, not letting me leave the booth. "I don't know what's going on, but I'm sorry. I didn't mean to make you feel like what you say doesn't matter to me because it does."

"Let. Me. Out." I couldn't stay there a moment longer. "Now."

"Ember, please."

"Now."

Getting up, he sighed. "Call me when you cool off, okay?"

I walked away without answering him. But when I got to Madison, I found her smiling and happy. "Mom, look at all the tickets I got."

I forgot about the tickets. "That's great, honey. Let's get them and go pick out some prizes to trade them with. It's time to get going."

I didn't want to face Cohen again, but my kid needed the tickets, so I had to do it. As I turned around to head back to the table for the forgotten tickets, I found them on the table, but Cohen was gone.

My heart slammed against my chest, knowing I'd run him off. The war my mind and body were waging made me feel insane. Part of me wanted to chase after him and tell him the truth about everything. But the other part told me to let him go — it was all for the best.

"Hey, where's Cohen?" Madison grabbed the tickets off the table as she looked around.

Unbelievable calmness washed over me for some crazy reason. "Oh, he had to go. He had work to get to. He said to tell you bye, though." I took her hand, hating myself for telling another God-forsaken lie.

CHAPTER 17
COHEN

The disturbing way Ember had acted at the pizza place dampened my mood. I couldn't focus on anything, so I went home. After a long shower meant to cleanse away some of the pain, I still felt horrible.

I pushed too hard — that's gotta be it.

As much as it didn't feel like the right thing to do, I had to back off. At least for a while. I couldn't explain the way she had acted that way other than that I'd put too much pressure on her.

I may have only dated Ember for a week back then, but I'd known her for a little over a year before that. And she'd never acted like this back then. From her reactions, it seemed like this was new for her too.

At only seven in the evening, I got into bed. I'd never been so out of sorts in my life. Even after my parents had died. At least I knew they weren't coming back, and there was nowhere to move but forward.

With Ember, though, it felt like whiplash. She was telling me all the right things one minute, then she was pulling away the next. Confusion, worry, a fair amount of hurt feelings, and some anger simmered inside me.

The bottom line — Ember is being shitty.

She'd said, straight out, that if she'd known that I owned the resort, she would've given the trip away to someone else. To think that she would go to such lengths to avoid seeing me bothered me more than anything else.

Why would she not want to see me again?

Sure, running into someone you'd dumped was never easy. I'd had my fair share of run-ins with women I'd ended things with. And none of those reunions ever went well. But there wasn't any open hostility the way there was with Ember.

The thing was that Ember and I hadn't argued about what she wanted back then. I wasn't in agreement with her reasoning for ending things, and I let her know that. But I couldn't very well ignore the way she felt.

If being with me would somehow make her unhappy or cause her problems, I wouldn't have wanted things to go on either. So, I'd let her go with a kiss and a hug and told her that I wished her nothing but the best.

Ember had made me a better man. When I was with her, at least. I'd never met another woman who'd made me want to be a better person. And even though she was acting so out of character now, she still had that effect on me. I wanted to do right by her — however, she needed me to.

So, instead of arguing or trying to make her see reason, I just left. I'd also told her to call me when she calmed down. Five hours had passed with no call, though, and I was fairly sure she'd calmed down within that timeframe.

She simply doesn't want you, bro.

With a deep sigh, I placed my hands under my head, staring at the ceiling. No matter what my subconscious said, I knew she still wanted me. She'd proven that already.

The problem was her daughter. She didn't want her daughter to witness anything that she might take back home and talk about. Ember would've been more than happy to stay in my arms and my bed if her daughter wasn't with her.

Again, I understood her motives. I didn't agree with them, but I did understand them. If Madison went back telling tales about me and her mom being all over each other, kissing, hugging, and that kind of thing, her family would be upset with Ember.

To me, upsetting someone wouldn't be enough for me to push away the only person I'd ever had a chance of falling in love with. I didn't have a kid, though. And I didn't depend on those people, who would be upset, to help me take care of my kid. So, I understood a little — but I thought Ember was being too stubborn. After all, I'd given Ember another option. If she took me up on it, she wouldn't need anyone in her family to take care of Madison.

Wanting to drown out my thoughts, I turned on a random podcast. The topic was allergies, and they were talking to a scientist who was explaining how a lot of research showed that some allergies – especially shellfish allergies – could be genetic.

A thought sprang into my head. I picked up my cell off the nightstand and called my oldest brother, Baldwyn. He answered on the third ring, "What's up?"

"Hello to you too." I chuckled as I knew my brother was a busy man. The resort, his wife, and his kid made him that way. "How are Sloan and Audrey Rose doing this evening?"

"Sloan's in the kitchen, fixing dinner," he said with a laugh. "She's on a health-kick and insists on making all our meals from scratch. It's been two days so far, and I think this dinner will be the end for her. She's cussing up a storm in there as we speak. And Audrey Rose is playing with some of her dolls and having a tea party with them in front of the television. And what's going on with you?"

"Not much. I'm staying in tonight — doing some thinking."

"You?" he sounded surprised. "It's Saturday night. Are you aware of that, Cohen?"

"Yes, I'm aware of that. I'm just not in the mood to go out."

"Feeling sick?"

"No." *Heartsick.* But I didn't want to get into that with him. "I have a question for you. It's about Mom."

I didn't know a hell of a lot about Ember's family. But I did know that both she and her sister, Ashe, loved seafood. So, that had me wondering where Madison's allergy to shellfish had come from. And a distant memory wouldn't leave my head. I wasn't sure I was recalling things correctly, so that's why I called my oldest brother to verify my memory.

"About Mom?"

"Yeah." We didn't talk a lot about our parents. It had been such a long time since their deaths that it made it hard to bring them up sometimes. "You feel like you can talk about her right now?"

"Yeah, I can talk about her. What do you want to know about Mom?"

"I sort of remember us eating shrimp one sunny afternoon. We were in our backyard, and Dad was grilling them on the barbeque pit. And he'd said that we were only getting to enjoy them that day because Mom had gone to spend the weekend with her aunt to take care of her after some sort of surgery or something like that." I'd never completely understood why that was. "So, why'd he say that?"

"Mom was allergic to shrimp — that's probably why. She was so allergic to them that we couldn't even have them in the house, or she'd break out in hives. I guess she was allergic to all shellfish, but Dad only ever brought up the shrimp because he loved them but could hardly ever eat them because of her allergy."

Allergic to shellfish — just like Madison.

"Did anyone else in our family have that same allergy that you know of?"

"Mom said that her grandmother on her mother's side had

the same reaction when she got anywhere near shrimp. But she also said that her mom didn't have the allergy and ate shrimps all the time. She thought it might be the sort of thing that skips a generation. We had Audrey Rose tested for the allergy already, and she's good. But the pediatrician said that it could develop at any time. So, we have to be careful about her and what she eats, just to be on the safe side."

"Do Patton and Warner know about that since they've got kids now?" My brothers and I didn't talk about the intricacies of everything that affected their kids, so I had no idea if any of my nieces or nephews had the allergy.

"Yeah, I made sure to tell them about it so they could inform their pediatricians. Charlotte Grace has the allergy, but Patton's boys don't."

"Sounds like the girls get it easier than the boys."

"I've got no idea how things like that work. I'm just glad that my daughter hasn't shown any signs of that so far. Allergies like that are no joke. One bite of the thing can swell their throats up to the point of closing, and then the kid can't breathe. It's that serious."

"Shit, sounds scary." I wouldn't wish that on anyone – especially not a kid. "Thankfully, people with severe allergies can carry something called an EpiPen – it pumps them full of adrenaline to counteract the reaction. But why are you asking about this anyway? Are you having a reaction to something you ate?"

"No." I didn't want to get into it with him. We all still had friends back home in Houston. One never knew who might accidentally say something in passing that might get back to Ember's family. *She'll kill me if that happens.* "I just was thinking about Mom was all."

"Oh. That's kind of weird because we've never really done anything about Mom's and Dad's birthdays — but today would have been her fifty-ninth birthday. Funny that you're thinking about her on this day. Maybe that means she's close to you right now."

The idea made something spark inside of me. "Yeah, that is weird. Thanks for filling me in. And tell Sloan and Audrey Rose that I said hi and I love 'em. Night, Baldwyn. I love you too, big brother."

"Night, Cohen. Love you too, bro."

As I placed the phone back on the nightstand, I looked around the dimly lit room. "Mom, you here?" I would normally feel stupid talking to a dead person, but I had the feeling that she might be hanging around me for some reason.

Listening for the slightest sound, I didn't hear a thing. Another idea came to me. I picked up my phone again and went straight to social media. I searched for Ember and found some pictures of her with Madison.

One of them piqued my interest quite a bit. A birthday cake that was lit up with six candles and Madison blowing them out. I checked the date and saw that it was posted in April of this year. And the comments were all wishing Madison a happy birthday.

Madison turned six this year.

I hadn't asked about Madison's age as it had never occurred to me to do such a thing. But now that I knew she was six years old and had been born in April, something tickled at my brain.

Seven years ago, Ember and I had spent one magical week together at the end of July — nine months before April.

My head grew so light that if I hadn't been lying down, I might've fallen over. If what I thought were true, then it might explain Ember's behavior. When a wild animal is backed into a corner, it will not come out without a fight. Maybe Ember felt as if she'd been backed into an impossible corner, and that's why she was lashing out at me.

Could that little girl be my daughter?

CHAPTER 18
EMBER

Sleep evaded me the entire night as I sat up, worrying that Cohen might burst into the room. He had said that he wouldn't let me go without a fight this time, and I believed him.

I packed our things while Madison slept soundly, wanting to be ready to leave as soon as she woke up. But when five a.m. rolled around, and she hadn't even stirred a little, I began making some noises so she'd wake up.

Pulling the luggage cart into the room, I heaved our bags onto it, making sure to grunt and clang metal against metal. My efforts paid off as she sat up, rubbing her eyes. "Mom! What the heck are you doing?"

"Oh, did I wake you up? Sorry, honey. It's just that we've got to get on the road. I've got so much to do before I head out to work this evening. I've gotta buy you some sneakers, remember? And then I've gotta do the laundry and pack my work clothes and your clothes for the two weeks you'll be at your grandparents'."

She lay back down. "Mom, it's still dark outside. We can't leave yet."

"Yes, we can. I've got you some clean clothes in the

bathroom. I need you to get up and change out of your nightgown so I can tuck it into the bag of dirty laundry, and then we'll hit the road." I went to bed, urging her to get out of as I pulled the blankets back. "Come on, sweetie. Let's get going now."

"It's way too early, Mom." She flipped onto her side so that she didn't have to look at me. "Anyway, I want to tell Cohen goodbye, and he probably isn't here yet."

I couldn't take another encounter with Cohen Nash. "Sweetie, he said that he wouldn't be coming into work today because it's Sunday, and he never works on Sunday. So, there's no reason to wait. Come on now, get up."

Sitting up, she looked at me with squinty eyes. "Well, call him, and we can meet him somewhere so we can tell him goodbye. I don't wanna leave without saying goodbye. And I want to know when we're coming back here too."

Never.

Being that she was just a kid, I had high hopes that she would just forget about the resort and Cohen over a relatively short amount of time. "Well, I'll have to see how work goes before I can figure out anything like when we can come back. And Cohen must have other things to do today because he didn't say anything about wanting to meet up before we left town. He's a busy man, you know."

"Maybe he goes to church on Sundays." She nodded as she got out of bed and trod toward the bathroom on wobbly legs. "If he woulda told us which church he goes to, then we coulda went too."

"Yep. Your clothes are on the vanity." It was way too early for Cohen to just show up, but that didn't keep the nerves from getting to me. "Hurry, okay?"

Ignoring me, Madison took her time, and it was nearly six before she came out of the bathroom. "Can you brush my hair?"

I ran the brush through her hair quickly then pulled it back in a ponytail. "There you go. Put on your shoes, and let's get going."

Slipping her feet into her shoes, she sighed as she took one last look around the luxurious suite. "Man, I'm really gonna miss this place."

"Yes, I can see that. But we've got to get home. I'm sure your grandparents miss you."

Shuffling along behind me, Madison was quiet as we left the place she'd come to love so much in such a short amount of time. The lobby was dim as we passed through. I left the baggage cart with the rest of them at the door and grabbed our bags.

Madison tugged the bottom of my shirt. "Mom, can we tell someone to let Cohen know we said goodbye?"

"I already told him goodbye yesterday, so that's not necessary." I walked out the door as it opened and looked back in time to see her picking up a pamphlet before following me. "I got this thing that says stuff about the resort. I wanna show it to my teacher at school to show her where we went this weekend."

"K, let's go then." I'd parked as close as I could to the door since I knew we'd be leaving as early as possible. Popping the trunk with my key fob, I tossed the luggage in then closed it before letting Madison into the back seat and buckling her into her booster seat. "There you go."

She stared at the pamphlet in her hand. "Mom, I feel like I'm really gonna miss this place and Cohen. I feel like I might cry." She looked at me with shining eyes. "Are you sure that we can't go tell him goodbye? You have his phone number, right?"

"No." I did have his card in my purse, but she didn't know that. "Even if I did have it, I wouldn't call him this early. That would be rude."

"I think it's rude of us to leave without saying goodbye."

I closed the backdoor, my heart aching.

My daughter was about to cry over a man she shouldn't

have felt that close to. She shouldn't have caught feelings for Cohen this fast. It made me wonder if she felt a connection to him in some way.

I wonder if Cohen felt a connection to her too.

Shaking off the idiotic notion, I got into the car and drove away, feeling relieved as I left the parking lot. Now we could get back home and our normal schedule. This whole thing with Cohen would fade away in time.

The guilt that racked me might not fade as quickly, but I had to hope that it *would* fade. A whole new set of problems had risen out of our visit to Austin.

I was no longer worried about how upset my sister and parents would be at me for being with Cohen. The bigger worry was how my daughter would feel if she ever found out how much and how long I'd lied to her. And then there was Cohen to worry about too. He'd hate me if he knew what I'd done.

Seeing Cohen with hate for me in his eyes would kill me. And the disappointment I was sure would come from Madison's eyes would finish me off.

All this time, I'd thought the worst part was upsetting my family. Now I knew there was something far worse than that. And I had no idea how I could right all the wrongs I'd done.

"School's gonna be out for summer soon. Maybe you can take a vacation from work, and we can come back to the resort."

"I can't afford to stay there, honey. We couldn't even have stayed this time if my company hadn't paid for it."

"Cohen would let us stay for free."

"We can't impose on his good nature like that."

"Yes, we can, Mom."

My hands gripped the steering wheel so hard that my knuckles turned white. I couldn't argue with her about this. "We'll see," I said.

She sniffled, and I looked in the rearview mirror, catching her wiping her eyes with her hands.

She's crying.

My stomach began to hurt as tears burned the backs of my eyes. I hadn't ever wanted anything like this to happen. It was never even on my radar that this sort of thing could happen — even if we ever were to run into Cohen.

My kid was crying over having to leave her father – without even knowing he was her father. Maybe their blood just called to each other.

How's Cohen going to feel when he finds out that we're gone?

If Madison felt sad about not getting to say goodbye — would Cohen feel that way too?

Who am I kidding? Of course he's going to be sad that he didn't get to say goodbye.

As I pulled onto the highway, a chill ran through me. I hadn't given Cohen my phone number or address, but he had access to it through the resort.

I've gotta change my phone number. And I might have to move too. Shit!

One little trip, and my life seemed to be turning upside down. And the only one to blame for that fiasco was myself. For the first time since I found out that I was pregnant, I felt like I should've confided in at least one person who could've helped me make better decisions.

Keeping secrets from the entire world was cumbersome, to say the least. But the guilt that kept building inside of me might prove to be something that could destroy me.

I kept feeling like I needed a drink to help calm my nerves — and that was worrying. Booze wouldn't change a thing, except my state of mind. It might help me temporarily forget what I'd done, but it wouldn't erase anything.

"He's gonna miss us, Momma," she whimpered. "He's gonna be sad that we're gone. I know he will be."

Trying not to break down in front of her, I took a deep

breath. "Madison, he's got a lot to do at the resort. And he's got an active social life too, with lots of family and friends. Did you know that he's got four brothers?"

"No. He didn't tell me that." She took the napkin I held out to her and wiped her nose.

"He's got plenty of people in his life already. I'm not saying he won't miss you cause you're a great kid, but he won't be lonely."

"He's gonna miss *you* too, Mom. He likes you a lot. I think you like him too, even though you won't say so."

"Sure, I like him. But as a friend. Nothing more than that."

She picked up the pamphlet and held it against her heart. "I won't ever forget."

God, she's making this so much harder than I thought it would be.

CHAPTER 19

COHEN

I walked into the lobby of Whispers Resort right at eight a.m. and headed towards the elevator. I wasn't going to let Ember dodge my questions, but I knew I had to get Madison out of earshot before I began asking anything.

Knocking three times, I called out, "Ember? Maddy?"

I did not hear anything. I knew Ember might not answer the door, but Madison would've opened it no matter what her mother said. Looking down the hallway, I saw one of the maid carts at the very end, as the cleaning had already begun.

After borrowing her master keycard, I went back and swiped it, opening the door to find that all their things were gone. "Shit!"

Ember hadn't given me her number, and I hadn't gotten Madison's either. I went back and gave the master keycard to the maid, then went down to the lobby.

I could find Ember's phone number and address through our registry system, but I knew that would be violating our policies – and her privacy. I'd left the business card with my personal phone number on it in their room that first night; I just had to hope that Ember would call me.

I headed over to Baldwyn's, needing to talk to someone

about my suspicions. Who better than my big brother? Being a Sunday morning, I expected his home to be quiet, but it was anything but that as I rang the bell and Audrey Rose flung the door wide open. "Uncle Cohen!" She jumped into my arms, hugging me like she hadn't seen me in a year. But I'd just seen her a few days earlier.

"Well, good morning to you, Miss Audrey Rose."

I put her down, and she turned to run inside, announcing my arrival, "Uncle Cohen's here! Uncle Cohen's here!"

Following her, I found the small family in the kitchen making breakfast. Sloan had a carton of eggs on the counter. "You're going to eat breakfast with us."

"That didn't sound like a question." I took a seat next to my brother. "But I accept your gracious invitation."

She poured a cup of coffee then put it in front of me. "Organic – from the rain forest. You try it."

"If you insist." I leaned over to whisper to my brother, "I think she's had a cup or two already."

His nod confirmed my suspicions. "Take it slow on that liquid energy."

"Organic bacon, farm-fresh eggs, and I'm trying my hand at homemade flour tortillas. Audrey Rose, come help me, please."

"Sure, Momma." She shimmied up on a barstool to help.

"While they're busy with breakfast, can you and I talk in private?" What I wanted to talk about was a discussion better left to adults.

"Yep." He took his cup of coffee, and I grabbed mine, then we went to his mancave. "What's up?"

I took a seat on one of the many comfy recliners as he took the one nearest to me. "Baldwyn, I have reason to believe that I might be a father."

He looked surprisingly calm at what I thought would've been shocking news. With a heavy sigh, he looked me in the eye. "Cohen, I'm not gonna lie to you. Sharing a child with someone isn't easy. And you never stay with any woman long enough to get to the tough shit. So, who is this woman that you've knocked up?

I smiled as I thought about just how compatible I was with Ember — when she wasn't being as prickly as a hedgehog. "If I'm right, then I have knocked her up seven years ago."

He adjusted himself as his eyes went wide. "Are you saying that you might have been the first one among us to become a father?"

"Maybe." I knew that was blowing his mind since they loved to joke that I was the least likely to ever grow up.

"That is very interesting, Cohen. And the mother of this kid never contacted you then? Did she just tell you about this?" He held up one finger as he had a point to make. "Because she might be after your money. You would need to deal with her through a lawyer, not on your own – just to be safe."

"She's not that way. And she hasn't told me anything at all. You remember Ashe Wilson from my early twenties, right?"

"Leggy blonde, bossy attitude. Lasted one or two months?" He nodded. "She's the one, then?"

"No. It's her younger sister, Ember."

His jaw got tight. "Cohen, no, no, no. You did not screw one of your ex-girlfriend's sisters. Tell me it's not true. Tell me you did not get your ex's little sister pregnant seven years ago. This could cost you a bundle."

"Listen, Baldwyn." I had no idea he'd be so cynical about this. "Ember and I were only together for about a week. But it was an incredible time. It's the closest thing I've ever come to love. Actual love." I stared at him hard, hoping he'd see the depth of my feelings on the topic. "She and her daughter came to the resort after her company gave her the trip. She told me she'd felt the same. That she'd come close to falling in love with me all those years ago too."

"Wow." He rolled his eyes. "If it's all lovey-dovey between

you two, then why didn't she tell you about the kid seven years ago?"

"She never told her family about us – and they were the reason she broke things off in the first place. She didn't want to upset them. I think that she kept the identity of the father a secret from them this whole time. With the baby, she must've been scared to death to tell them that I was the father." I felt sort of sorry for her about all that too.

"Where are they now?" He looked very serious, like he'd hop in the car to go meet them if he could.

"I think they went back to Houston already."

"You think?" He shook his head. "Cohen, if you think you've got a kid, then you need to find that out for sure. Even if this Ember woman thinks her family will be mad at her, that doesn't matter, not even a little. What matters is being able to have a relationship with your kid. You said she has a daughter, right?"

"Yeah."

"So, you might have a daughter — just like me?"

"I might. And she's so adorable." I took out my cell and showed him a picture of Madison dancing at the pizza place the day before. "See. And she's so formal at times too. It's so funny. She tells her mom not to be rude and silly things like that – like a little adult."

Baldwyn took my phone and stared at the picture. "You should see something." He handed me the phone, then got up and returned with his laptop. "I joined this ancestry website and found some pictures of our parents. Since all the pictures we had were burned in the fire, I hoped to find some that our relatives had posted."

Passing me the computer, I immediately realized what he wanted me to see. "This little girl looks a lot like Madison."

"That little girl is our mother, Cohen. And these two little girls share the same nose and rosebud lips." He looked at my hair. "And the little girl in your picture has the same hair as your."

I couldn't help but get all tingly inside as it became clearer and clearer to me that Madison was indeed my daughter. "Baldwyn, I really might be a father!"

"Man, it sure looks like you might be." He eyed me. "So, what are you gonna do about this?"

"I'm going to talk to Ember and get the truth out of her. That's what I'm gonna do." I got up, ready to head out on a mission to get to the bottom of things.

"Breakfast is ready," Sloan called out. "Get in here while it's hot."

"After breakfast. I can't leave without eating what your lovely and talented wife has made."

"You sure as hell can't." He came up beside me, clapping me on the back. "I won't tell anyone about this until you know for sure."

"Yeah, keep it under wraps until I've got concrete evidence." I just hoped that once the truth was out, Ember would come to her senses.

If Madison was mine, I wouldn't want to raise her any other way than with her mother. It wasn't in me to take a kid away from their mother and a family who loved them. And I prayed Ember would feel the same about taking her away from me and my family.

Though she didn't seem to have cared about that for the last seven years.

I shook off the less than kind thought. She'd been young and scared when she got pregnant, and I definitely hadn't been dad material back then. There was no point in dwelling on the past, on things that couldn't be changed. My time and energy would be better spent on planning for the future.

Getting ahead of myself, I tried to stop thinking about anything other than my brother, his wife, and their little girl. Life still seemed fleeting to me, and I tried to be present in every golden moment I was given. Breakfast — made from scratch – with a family who I loved was a golden moment for sure.

"Sloan, these flour tortillas are almost as good as Joe's tacos downtown." I scooped up another helping of scrambled eggs with a chunk of tortilla and popped the bite into my mouth.

"Who do you think I got the recipe from?" Sloan winked at me. "All it cost me was a weekend stay at the resort, but I got the flour tortilla and the corn tortilla recipes. I think it was a bargain, to be honest."

"The only recipe he won't give — no matter what we've offered — is that green sauce of his," Baldwyn added. "I can't find anything that will make him give that recipe up."

Sloan got up and went to the fridge. "I'm glad you brought that up. He wouldn't give me the recipe, but he did give me a big bottle of the stuff." She doused her eggs with some, then passed it to my side of the table.

"What a treat," I said as I put a fair amount on my eggs too. "What a way to start a perfect Sunday."

"Glad you joined us, Cohen." Baldwyn smiled at me with knowing eyes. "Maybe this Sunday will be an exceptionally great one for you."

"Yeah, who knows?" I bit into a crispy piece of bacon and let out a moan as it melted in my mouth. "Who knew organic bacon could be so good?"

Sloan raised her hand. "I did."

After the hearty breakfast, I drove back to the resort. I knew that I had to find out Ember's phone number so I could ask her some tough questions.

Coming into the lobby, I headed to the front desk, knowing I was about to make some rather unscrupulous moves. Cameron came out from the back room and smiled as he saw me. "Hey there, Mr. Cohen. I've got a message back here for you."

My heart skipped a beat. I was sure the message was from

Ember. *Maybe she left me her phone number so I wouldn't have to snoop through her registration information after all.*

He slid a post-it note across the desk to me. "A little girl called just a little while ago. She said it was very important to make sure you got this message as soon as possible."

So, not Ember.

But it was just as good – it was from Madison. *From my daughter?* My chest felt tight, and my eyes stung, but I shook the feeling off. I didn't want to get my hopes up.

I shook my head, laughing internally at myself. Who would've thought I'd be so thrilled at the possibility of having a kid? *Definitely not me.*

Getting back to the task at hand, I looked down at the message. It said that she felt really, really bad for leaving without saying goodbye. It said to call her if I felt like saying goodbye. And her phone number was on it.

Taking the paper, I went back out to my truck with a massive smile on my face and made the call. "Hello?" she answered right away.

My heart swelled just from hearing her voice. "Hi, Maddy. It's me, Cohen."

"I'm glad you called. Mom had to get back here to Houston to get everything done so she could get to work for the nightshift. She doesn't know I left you a message."

"That's okay. I'm glad you did. I wanted to tell you goodbye too. Add this phone number to your contacts list so you can call me whenever you want to, okay? I had a great time with you guys this weekend. Did your mom give you any idea when you are coming back?"

"No. I'm sorry. I asked about coming back this summer, but she said she can't afford it."

My stomach sank, but I wasn't surprised. Ember had made it clear that she had no intentions of ever coming back to the resort, and probably not even to Austin for fear of running into me again.

"Well, you know I'd let you guys stay for free."

"I told her that, but she said she couldn't let you do that. She's lonely, Cohen. And she's afraid Aunt Ashe would get mad at her if she liked you for more than a friend. *Do* you like her for more than a friend?"

"Madison, your mom has only done what she thinks is best for you. Remember that."

I have to try to remember that too.

CHAPTER 20
EMBER

The two-hour drive to work gave me time to think. And I found that wasn't a good thing. Thinking only gave my conscience time to chew me out for being so dishonest with everyone I cared about. But it had more to torment me about, not only that. Getting between my daughter and her father seemed to be an even bigger sin — at least in my heart.

As soon as I got to the rig, I checked in with the company man, then headed to the mud-logging trailer to see how Roger's day had gone. "Evening, Roger." I closed the door behind me, putting a damper on the loud noises the oil rig made. "How's day one?"

"Not so good, Emmy." He liked to give everyone a nickname, just like so many others in the oilfield.

He handed me a paper he'd scribbled something on. "What's this?"

"I need you to take that to Slow Pete in the company trailer. He wants updates within a half-hour after each sample we catch and clean. This one's good — a hell of a lot better than the first eleven."

"You're doing a sample each hour?" That meant this was

going to not only be a dicey well, but it could last much longer than two weeks.

"We are." He nodded as he pointed at the door. "Go on now, get that to him, and I'll catch you up as soon as you get back."

Taking the note to Slow Pete, I walked as fast as I could, trying to step over the dozens of extension cords and water lines without tripping.

One of the guys on the rig crew pointed at me then at his hardhat, and I realized that I'd forgotten to put mine on. I hurried back to my car to grab it, then got going back the way I'd come.

When I opened the door, I found Slow Pete, Fat Manny, and a guy they called Cornbread looking at me. "'Bout time." Slow Pete took the scribbled note out of my hand. "I expect to get these updates as quickly as you can get them to me — which should be a hell of a lot quicker than this, Emmy."

"Yes, sir. I just got here. It's still a half-hour until I start my shift."

His eyes darted to mine as he looked up from the note that I couldn't even decipher. "Did I ask for an excuse?"

"No, sir." I crammed my hands into the pockets of my loose-fitting slacks. "Will that be all?"

"Yeah."

I turned to leave when Fat Manny asked, "How was the resort?"

My shoulders slumped, and I just nodded. "Good."

"Just good?" he asked. "That place cost a small fortune, and it was just good?"

"No." I turned to face him. "It was very nice, and the service was beyond my wildest imagination. The food, the accommodations, and the atmosphere were all amazing. Thanks for the trip. My daughter and I enjoyed it so much that it was hard for us to leave — especially for my kid. She loved everything about Whispers Resort and Spa. You definitely should keep giving out trips to that place as incentives and prizes."

"Glad to hear that. You're the first one to go. It's nice to know we've got a winning prize now. It's hard to please everyone with the incentives we give."

"Yeah, it's a great one." I had to get back to Roger to get briefed before I took over. "See you guys in about an hour."

When I got back, I found Roger sitting at the drafting table, drawing the log. "Well, did you find out what all the fuss is about, Emmy?"

"They didn't tell me a thing. So, fill me in." I sat at the table across from him and grabbed a pen and a paper off the side so I could take notes.

"I found bits of igneous rock in the third sample."

"Well, that's not good." I'd just been boasting during the weekend that I'd never had a well blow out on me, and here I was on a well that had pulled up volcanic rock material. "So, we've got to watch out for draws of magma and gas pockets with this one. Great."

"Hence the slow drilling speed and the need for hourly samples. The company men have big decisions to make with each sample we catch and clean, and that's why they want updates so quickly and so often."

"It's going to be a long night." And I hadn't had time to even catch a quick nap. Adding in the previous night of no sleep, I was in for a world of hurt.

Most first nights were so calm that I could usually catch a few winks of sleep throughout the night. This one was not going to go that way at all.

At least with the danger-factor, my adrenaline might help me stay awake until the end of my shift at seven in the morning.

True to what I'd anticipated, I worked my ass off that night. As soon as Roger showed his face out of the back room, I was ready to get my ass to bed. "Thank God. I'm bushed."

"You look like hell, Emmy." He started a pot of coffee as I

wrote down an update, then went to take it to the company man. "I'll be right back, and then I'm taking a shower and going to bed."

"I've got this. No worries."

Walking over to the other trailer, I stumbled over some electrical lines and nearly fell. "Fuck!"

Exhaustion didn't make it easy to traverse the plethora of tripping hazards. But I made it to the trailer to find a new guy there. One I hadn't met yet. "Hi, I'm Ember. Well, they call me Emmy around here. And you are?"

He looked at me as if I was some kind of an idiot as I held out the paper to him. "What makes you think I want that?"

"Um, you're a company man, right?"

"I'm the owner of Stanton Oil and Gas, not just a company man." He looked at his expensive watch then back at me. "And your update is five minutes late."

"Yes, I know it is. I'm very sorry. There's nothing pressing going on right now anyway. We haven't found anything in the last six hours to be worried about."

"Did I ask you for your opinion about what needs to be worried about?" He grabbed the paper out of my hand. "Go back to your trailer. And try to remember that you're a grunt around here, not one of the scientists who are trained and paid to tell me when to worry or when not to."

"Nice to meet you too." I turned and walked away, trying not to let the jackass turn me into a Tasmanian devil who would destroy everything in her path.

Muttering curse words under my breath, I went back to the trailer then stomped back into the bunkroom. "Did it go that bad?" Roger asked, picking up on my mood.

"No. But the asshole owner had to be a prick about things." I slid the door to the little room closed, then held my fists up in the air. "Ugh!"

One phone call would change my entire life, yet here I was, taking shit from an arrogant fool. And for what? Money?

Sitting down on the bottom bunk, I knew I needed money. But I knew there was more than one way to make it. So, I decided to do something crazy. I called my sister.

"Hello," she said groggily.

"You were still asleep?"

"It's seven in the morning, so yeah, I was still asleep. What's up, Ember?"

"I'm having a rough morning with the jerks around here. And I wanted to talk to you about something that happened this weekend at that resort we went to."

"Mom told me that Cohen Nash owns it. That's wild, alright."

"Well, he doesn't own it alone. He and his brothers own it. But yeah, that's wild."

"Mom said Madison keeps talking about him. How much time did you spend with him?" She already sounded annoyed.

I trod lightly. "Not much. You know how he is, he kept showing up – at least that much about him hasn't changed. And Madison was drawn to his charms like most women are."

"Yeah. He can draw them in; he just can't seem to keep any of them." She laughed at her little joke.

More like he hasn't wanted to keep any.

He did want to keep me, though. "Well, the thing I wanted to talk to you about was this job he offered me." Although that wasn't exactly true. He hadn't offered me a for sure job, but I had to make it sound like he had, or she would've asked far too many questions about why he wanted to give me a job in the first place.

"Oh, God!" her tone said it all. She thought he was up to something. "I bet he's just trying to get to your goods, Ember. He would do that just to get under my skin too. You know, just to pour salt into the wound he caused when he broke up with me."

"So, you don't think he could really like me?" I clamped my hand over my mouth for even saying that out loud – and to her, of all people. A job offer from a former acquaintance didn't have to mean anything, as far as anyone else was concerned.

"Ember, the man I knew was incapable of genuinely liking anyone. Surely you know that from what you saw him put me through." She huffed noisily. "What kind of job did the hero offer you? A position with the cleaning staff?"

"No." I knew she wasn't ever going to be okay with the truth. And I knew my family would have a fit if I told them I was taking Madison to go live in Austin and work at the resort. And telling them that we'd be staying in Cohen's guesthouse would only fuel their fire. "It was something with guest security."

I suddenly realized just how ridiculous this all was. She was still mad about a breakup that happened seven years ago – with a guy she'd only dated for a couple months! And he hadn't done anything more egregious than not wanting to be with her.

"But, you know, you haven't even talked to the man in seven years," I said, testing the waters to see how she'd react.

She huffed. "Men like him don't change, Ember. If he's not doing it to get in your pants, then he's probably doing it to hurt *me.*"

I rolled my eyes. Somehow everything always had to be about her. If that's what she still thought after all these years, I knew there'd be no reasoning with her.

CHAPTER 21
COHEN

A week passed without hearing from Ember or Madison. I could've asked Madison for her mother's phone number, but I had chosen not to. Calling her while she was working didn't seem like the right or smart thing to do. Not that I knew when the perfect time would be to ask her if I was Madison's father.

Not a day had gone by that I hadn't thought about them both — no matter how busy I'd been with work. I couldn't say that about anyone else I knew or had known. Ember and I had something special. I just needed her to realize that it was worth fighting for.

A quick knock on my office door took my attention, and then Baldwyn walked in. "I'm about to head home, and I thought I'd stop by to check up on you. How're you doing?"

Leaning back in my chair, I looked at the ceiling as I tried to find the right words. "Well, I'm kind of okay, but then I'm not."

Baldwyn came to my desk, leaning on it as he eyed me. "You look tired, and that's not like you."

"I wake up a lot at night. Not sure why that is, but it's been happening all week." I'd never had any trouble sleeping, so it has been quite an unusual week.

"You're stressed out over all this." He nodded, crossing his arms over his chest. "And you're mad at Ember too."

"Well, that's not exactly true, Baldwyn. I understand why she's done what she has. It's not like I was some kind of stand-up guy seven years ago when the whole thing went down. I can't even say what I would've done had she told me about the pregnancy back then. I was such a different person."

"You're right. You're not the same man you were seven years ago. And now you have the stability that you didn't before. You could be a good father — if she would just give you the chance to be one. She could've told you about this while she was here. But she chose not to."

I couldn't be that pissed at her no matter how hard I tried to be. "I know I'm probably not being true to my own feelings, but I just can't seem to stay angry with her over this. I've been rehashing things in my head for a whole week, and still, I find myself getting over the anger so quickly."

"Maybe it's best that you aren't that angry at her. Maybe you two can figure out a way to share your daughter. Well, if she is yours. You need to get a DNA test done."

I knew most people would think that, but the idea sort of bothered me. "Ember wasn't the kind of girl who had sex with lots of different guys — at least she wasn't like that back then. From what she said, she's still not that way. I don't wanna start out our family life with me not trusting her word."

His wide eyes told me he didn't agree with me. "She *lied* to you. You *can't* trust her."

I shook my head; I didn't feel the way I knew most people thought I should. "Let's be fair. I'm not sure Madison is mine. But if Ember tells me that she is, then I'm pretty sure I'll accept that as the truth. So, what I'm saying is that, at this time, I'm not looking to get a DNA test. But if Ember won't come clean or tells me that I'm not the father, then I'll ask for a test."

"That's better than nothing, I guess. How long are you

going to wait until you talk to her about this? Each day you wait is another day you'll lose with your daughter."

I had no idea how long I could keep waiting. "With the lack of sleep, and my mind darting to her and Madison so much of the time, I know I can't wait much longer."

"And you shouldn't," he said with a nod. "You need to do right by the kid — if she is yours. If she's a Nash, she should know it and be treated as well as her cousins. And she should meet her family."

"I don't think she's being mistreated at all, Baldwyn. Ember would never allow that to happen. I'm positive about that. But I agree with you. If Madison is mine, then I want her with me. Not that I'm about to try and take her from her mother. To be honest, I want them both with me."

One dark brow cocked as he asked, "What are you saying, Cohen? That you'd marry Ember if the kid is yours?"

"Marry?" I hadn't said that word. "Marriage is serious. I mean, I can't jump into a marriage just because I have a kid with someone. Even if that someone is incredibly special to me. Marriage is just too much to ask right now."

"Yeah, I agree. I was just asking. And by your reaction, I can see that you're not ready for such a crucial commitment." With a chuckle, he went to sit on the sofa. "You might never be ready for marriage. It's not all sunshine and rainbows. I can tell you that for sure."

I didn't like the way he was making me sound – like I was so immature or something. "I'm sure it's not all great."

"There are lots of ugly parts in marriage. You see each other at your worst – both mental and physical."

I didn't like the way he emphasized that last word. "I like Ember for her personality. I mean, she's hot and all, but it's her inner beauty that I really like."

"Wow." He looked stunned. "Are you being serious right now?"

"I mean it, Baldwyn. I think that in the past, I actively looked for imperfections – in appearances and personalities – of the women I dated to give me a reasonable excuse to end things without feeling guilty. But I've never done that with Ember. I know she's not perfect, but I don't care. I mean, I'm not perfect either."

"It's nice to hear you reflect on how you treated other women. I've often wondered if you knew that about yourself. Seems that you do now." Nodding, he smiled at me. "Cohen, could it be that this woman might have been the one that got away?"

I'd often thought so. "I think she might just be the one, period. How'd you know Sloan was the one for you?"

His smile grew in intensity as he took a walk down memory lane. "She's the only woman who made electricity run through my veins with nothing more than her touch."

That's what happens to me whenever Ember touches me.

"So, that never happened to you with anyone else? Not ever?"

He shook his head. "Not ever and not since. She's the one — always has been, I guess. It just took us a while to find each other."

"But I found Ember, and she dumped me." Maybe she'd lied to me about how I had made her feel back then.

"Yeah." He nodded.

"That's why I'm saying that marriage is more than I can think about right now. If I could get them to move into my guesthouse, I'd be satisfied. For a while anyway." My cell phone rang, and I pulled it out to find Madison's name on the screen. "It's Madison. I'd better take this." Swiping the screen, I answered, "Hey there, Maddy girl. How are you doing?"

All I heard back was a sob. "A girl at school called me names and told everyone I was a dummy who can't count to a hundred!" she whimpered.

"Honey, it's okay. Names can't hurt you."

"Yes, they can! I don't ever wanna go back to that stupid school with that mean girl. She's so mean, Cohen. She called me ugly cause the rubber band holding my ponytail broke, and my hair went everywhere. It was all wavy and stuff. She said I was so ugly."

I was immediately appalled. "And what did your teacher do?"

"She was out of the room and didn't hear anything. And I'm not a tattletale, so I didn't tell her. But I never wanna go back to that school again! Not ever!"

"Have you talked to your mom or your grandparents about this?" I was sure they would go to the teacher to let her know about the bullying that was going on.

"No. Mom's working, and Grammy had to take Gramps to the doctor today. I'm at Aunt Ashe's, but I don't wanna tell her cause she'll just tell me how I have to stand up to that mean girl. But I don't want to do that. I just don't want to ever see her again."

I couldn't believe she had called me and told me about this before she telling anyone else. I felt my heart grow, but I also felt the pressure of having to give her some good advice. "Look, sweetie, I know you don't want to stand up to her. And I get that you don't ever want to see her again. But you should understand some things about certain people. See, you're such a pretty little girl that some other girls will always be jealous of you. That's why that girl said those ugly things. She's jealous of you, and putting you down makes her feel better. But it's not right, and your teacher needs to talk to that girl's parents about her bad behavior, so they can correct her."

"Why would she be jealous of me? She's pretty too."

"Maybe she hasn't been told that. Maybe you should tell her that you think she's pretty and that you're going to forgive her for saying those things to you. You could tell her that you'd like to be friends with her."

"But that's not true. I don't want to be her friend now cause she's so mean." She sniffled, but the tears had dried up, so I knew she was already beginning to feel better.

"You're a nice person, Madison. I've seen you get along with people you've just met. You've got a good heart. I know you can do this. I know that you can find it in your heart to tell your Grammy about what's happened, so she can tell your teacher. Let the grownups handle what needs to be done about this girl. But you can let her know that you're not angry with her. Can you do that?"

"Well, I'm not mad at her. I'm just upset that she called me names and embarrassed me in front of the other kids." She blew her nose. "But you're right about letting the grownups handle things. And I'll tell Grammy about it. Mom won't be home until next Friday. She's gonna pick me up after school."

Next Friday?

"You sound a lot better, kiddo. I'll let you go for now, but you call me later if you want, after you tell your grammy about this."

"K, I will. I miss you, Cohen. I'm gonna try to talk Momma into coming to the resort when she returns home. Will that be okay with you?"

I knew Ember wouldn't do that. "Tell you what, I'll come up with an idea that might work. But let's keep that our little secret, k?"

"K. I'll call you later. And thanks. You made me feel a lot better."

"I'm glad you called me, Maddy. Bye now."

"Bye."

As I put the cell back into my pocket, I caught Baldwyn grinning. "I have to say that you've really surprised me."

My mind was busy working on how I could have some face-to-face time with Ember at the end of the coming week. "How's that?"

"Well, the way you talked to that little girl was very…

fatherly. Maybe you're more ready for this little family thing than I even realized."

"I know I'm ready. It's Ember I'm worried about."

CHAPTER 22
EMBER

Although I'd stayed up the whole night, I drove home as soon as Roger got up and took over the last shift. I couldn't wait to get the hell off of that rig. Plus, I couldn't wait to see my daughter.

Madison had called and talked to me about some girl who was bullying her at school, which had bothered me. I didn't like the idea of someone being mean to my kid. Thankfully, my mother went to the teacher, and things were resolved by the following day.

All I knew was that I wanted to spend the weekend spoiling my daughter. The guilt of having to leave her for such long periods was getting to me. I'd thought about calling Cohen every day since we'd left Austin.

Taking a job at the resort made perfect sense to me — even if my sister didn't agree. The only thing that worried me was that I was quite sure that Cohen was angry at me. I had no idea how he would take my call – if I could drum up the courage to make one.

I was still on the fence about everything, though. Decisions weren't coming easily to me. My heart wanted to right all my wrongs, but my ego knew it was going to take a beating when everyone found out that I'd lied for so long.

Just as I pulled into the apartment complex, my mother called. "I've just made it home, Mom," I answered the call.

"Good." She couldn't stop herself from checking up on me all the time. "How was traffic?"

"Awful, as usual. Houston traffic is a nightmare, and I think it'll always be that way." I parked the car in my usual parking space then grabbed my bag out of the backseat before heading into the apartment.

The thing about living in Pasadena was that no matter where my work took me, I always had to drive all the way through Houston to get to the suburb we lived in. "How come you and Dad had to pick this side of town to live in? It makes the drive so much worse."

"Oh, hush now. You're just grouchy because you haven't gotten any sleep yet. Have yourself a nice nap, and you'll feel much better. You *are* picking Madison up from school today, *right?*"

"Yes." I always picked my daughter up the day I came back from work. We'd go get an ice-cream from the Dairy Queen, then make our plans for how we'd spend my time off. "I've got a whole five days off before next job starts."

"Great," she said with tons of enthusiasm. "I'll tell your father that we can go on that fishing trip he's been wanting to. He'll be happy about that. With all his issues he's had to see the doctor about, it'll do him some good to get out of the house."

"Mom, why is he having to go to the doctor so often?" I went into the house, tossed my bag onto the sofa, then headed to my bedroom as I stripped off my clothes on the way. All I wanted to do was get naked and dive under the covers of my own bed and sleep for a few hours.

"I think it's the smog around here, to be honest. He's having allergy problems like crazy." She fell quiet for a moment, then added, "You know, it might be best for him if we found somewhere else to live. Somewhere without smog. A house in the country might be nice."

If they moved, then I would have to move too. "Oh. Well, yeah, that might be just what Dad needs." My father's health was more important than us having to relocate. But then Madison would have to change schools, and that would be an entire thing on its own.

That job at the resort just keeps looking better and better.

The time may have come for all of us to make some big changes. But I wasn't sure whether I was ready yet. And my daughter needed to be ready as well.

"I'm glad you understand, Ember. I've been worried about talking to you about this for some time now. I know Madison will have to change schools, and that would be a big adjustment for her. But, you know, kids are usually better at adjusting than adults." She sighed, and I could tell that this had been taking a toll on her. "I'm more worried about how your sister will take it if I'm honest. She can't uproot her family just to be closer to me and your father. Not that she should even consider doing that. But you know how she can make things all about her."

It seemed to me that the time may have come for us to start calling Ashe out on her behavior. "Mom, if Madison started acting the way Ashe does, I would be trying my best to correct that selfish behavior. Do you get what I'm saying?"

"I do get it, honey. I'm not blind to your sister's selfishness. But she's been that way for so long that I've just come to expect it from her. At some point, it just became easier to deal with it rather than confront it."

"That's not good, Mom." I needed to take my own advice where my sister was concerned. "She can't always have things her way. And our lives shouldn't be affected by what she thinks or wants."

"You're right. And we are going to do what's best for your father, no matter how she feels about us moving. But I should be honest with you too, Ember."

"Please do." I didn't want my mother to think that she couldn't be honest with me about anything. Even if I wasn't always honest with her.

"Honey, I think it's time that you started looking for a job that would allow you to be home longer. So you can take care of Madison more. She misses you so much when you're gone. I think this job is creating too much of a gap between you two."

And there it was. One more reason to do the right thing for my daughter. "Mom, it's funny that you brought that up because while we were at that resort a couple of weeks ago, Cohen Nash said he could get me a job there. And he said we could stay in his guesthouse — rent-free. There's a twenty-four-hour daycare at the resort too, so Madison would be…"

She cut me off, "Ember, hold on a minute. Can you really trust that man? That seems extremely generous of him – are you sure he won't expect certain things from you if he gives you a free place to live? The job might be okay, but you can't live in the man's guesthouse. You know how he was when he dated your sister."

I should've known she would say something like that.

I had no idea how I could tell my family that Cohen was Madison's father when all they remembered of him was the aloof womanizer of seven years ago. *Another brick in the wall that seems to keep growing taller and taller, separating me from the truth.*

"Well, I'm not jumping into anything, Mom. Besides, I spent some time with him when we visited, and I think he's grown up since then. But I'm exhausted, so I'll let you go now. I've gotta get some sleep, so I'll be bright-eyed and bushy-tailed when I pick Madison up."

"Just remember to talk to me before you go accepting any offers from that man, Ember. I know he's easy on the eyes, and he seems to have the ability to get women to do whatever he wants them to, but you have to think with your brain and not your body."

It wasn't so much my body that kept thinking of Cohen. It was my heart. "Yes, Mom. I'll call you later. You and Dad have plans to make for your fishing trip now."

"Yes, we do. Bye now."

"Bye, Mom." I ended the call, then fell face-first down on my bed, inhaling the fresh scent of my blanket. "Finally, no oily smell."

One of the worst things about working on an oil rig was the never-ending stench of oil. It seeped into everything. That's why I always ditched my clothes in the hallway before I got into my bedroom.

The sleep deprivation had me falling into a coma-like slumber up until the alarm on my phone woke me up. "Shit!"

I had been sure that I'd wake up before it went off. With only fifteen minutes to get ready before I had to leave to pick up Madison, I bounded out of bed and only had time for a quick shower.

Wet hair, no makeup, some old shorts, and a t-shirt were all I had time for. I slipped my feet into a ratty old pair of flip-flops, then hustled my ass out the door.

Waking up in that unexpected way had me sort of rattled. As I pulled up to the school, I felt on edge and took some deep breaths, trying to get myself under control. I never did well when I had to rush around.

I'd parked right up front so that Madison would see my car when she came out the double doors. There were three minutes to spare before the bell rang. When it did, the flood of kids began, and I had to search really hard to find the one kid who belonged to me.

Finally, I saw her coming out. I watched her look around, her eyes stopping on someone else before turning to me. She waved, then ran my way. But her eyes were elsewhere as she called out, "You came!"

"Who the hell is she talking to?" I watched her as she raced to a truck that was parked a few spaces over. Other cars were parked between us, stopping me from noticing the tall, chocolate-colored truck, which I instantly recognized. "No way!"

Jumping out of my car, I moved like lightning to get to Madison, who'd already jumped into his arms. She was giggling like it was the best day of her life. "I missed you, Cohen!"

"I missed you too, pumpkin." He hugged her as his eyes found mine.

"You son of a bitch!" I couldn't believe he'd shown up here.

Madison's head snapped as she looked at me with shocked eyes. "Momma!"

"Ember," Cohen said calmly. "I didn't come here to upset you."

"He came to surprise you, Mom," Madison said as he put her back on the ground.

"Oh, I'm surprised, alright." I took her hand, pulling her along with me.

"Ember?" I felt his hand on my shoulder.

As always, his touch sent electricity shooting throughout my body. "Get your fucking hand off me, Cohen Nash!"

"Mom!" Madison shouted. "Stop it!"

"It's okay, Maddy." He removed his hand, but my body still tingled. "I guess she's right to be mad at me for showing up without warning."

"You guess?" I knew I was making a scene, but I couldn't stop myself. "You fucking guess?"

There were too many thoughts rushing through my head. What would the teacher and the other parents think, seeing

Madison jump into this man's arms? A man who looked just a bit too much like my daughter.

They would think he was her father – and they would be right.

CHAPTER 23

COHEN

Ember's actions caught some teacher's attention, and she rushed toward us. "Excuse me! Excuse me, please!"

Ember's eyes blazed as she turned to look at the woman who had dared approach us. "What do you want?"

"For you to take this elsewhere, Miss Wilson." She looked at me with accusing eyes. "This is not the place for whatever is going on here. At least watch your language around the children."

"You're right," I said. "I'm sorry. We'll get going."

Ember pulled Madison with her as she went to her car. Madison's eyes were on me as she looked over her shoulder. "Follow us home, Cohen."

Nodding, I went to my truck and did as she'd asked, following them all the way to an apartment complex about a mile from the school. My heart kept pounding the way it had since the moment I set eyes on Ember as she charged towards me like a raging bull.

Being unsure of how she would take me following her home, I got ready for an argument. Parking beside her, I got out, squaring my shoulders for the fight I was sure was about to start. But I couldn't back down. This was for my daughter. Or at least, the daughter I hoped was mine.

I'd never hoped for a child in my life. But there I was, hoping and praying that I would soon find out that Madison was my little girl. And I had a ton of hope that Ember would want to raise her with me and that, one day, we'd become a real family — if I just played this right.

Instead of a fight, I watched Ember jump out of her car then sprint into the apartment. Madison got out of the backseat, looking at me with a half-smile. "That went well, didn't it?"

"I'm sorry about that, Madison. I didn't think your mom would be so mad at me for showing up, but now I see that I should have talked to her beforehand." I knew I should've called Ember. But there was a part of me that wanted to surprise her, thinking it would be romantic or something. That part of me had clearly been dead wrong.

"She's not mad anymore. I talked to her on the way home. Now, she's just embarrassed about the house being a mess and asked me to keep you out here for a few minutes to give her time to clean up." She leaned back against the car, crossing her arms over her chest. "So, how was the drive?"

She was such a little grownup. It was too cute. "It was fine. I checked into a hotel not far from here. It's got a swimming pool with lots of cool stuff, like slides and things like that. We'll have to talk your mom into bringing you over there so you can go swimming."

Her eyes lit up. "We sure will!" Reaching out, she took my hand. "Come on, she's had plenty of time to clean up now. I'm so glad you came. Even if my mom yelled and said all those bad words, I'm still glad you came to see us."

"I'd hate to be her at your next parent-teacher meeting," I joked. If I had my way, there would be no more parent-teacher meetings at that school.

This visit would put an answer to my question. Either

Ember would confirm that I was the father, or she'd tell me that I wasn't, in which case I would get a DNA test done. Either way, I wanted to let Ember know that I hadn't stopped thinking about her and us and how I wanted her to come to Austin — whether Madison was mine or not.

As soon as we stepped into the apartment, I noticed something right off the bat. The white walls were completely bare. There was not a single picture or a decoration of any kind adorning them.

"You can take a seat anywhere you'd like, Cohen. I'm going to go put my backpack in my bedroom, then I'll be right back."

"K." Scanning the place, I found it to be the least homey place I'd ever seen. One small sofa sat in front of a small television. A table for four, right by the tiny kitchen, was the only place with enough seating for all of us. So, I went and took a chair, waiting for them to come back out.

If Ember agreed to take me up on my offer, she and Madison would be a hell of a lot more comfortable living in my guesthouse than in this tiny apartment. Their lives would be so much richer in so many ways if Ember would only come to Austin.

Madison skipped down the hallway, smiling as she came my way. "I'm gonna see what's in the fridge to drink. You want something?"

"Sure." Ember's absence was noticeable. "Did you see your mom while you were back there?" I asked.

"She's in the bathroom." She opened the fridge then closed it. "Nothing's in there. Mom usually goes to the grocery store once she gets back from work. She must not have gone today, though."

"That's okay. I'm not really thirsty anyway."

"I am. But I can't reach the glasses." She came to the table and grabbed a chair, scraping it over the vinyl floor as she pulled it toward the kitchen.

Getting up, I took the chair from her and put it back in place. "How about I get a glass for you?"

"That would be nice. Thank you very much, Cohen. I just want some water." She went and took a seat at the table. "I don't like drinking out of the water fountains at school. Some kids play this mean trick where they come up behind kids drinking the water. Since they can't see them, they push their heads down so that their face gets all wet. And then everyone laughs at the poor kid who almost drowned."

"Yeah, I've seen that happen too. Can't blame you for not wanting that done to you." I opened the first cabinet that I came to. Four yellow plates, four clear glasses, and two green bowls were all that was in it. I took a glass and went to the sink to fill it with water. "You want some ice?"

"I don't think we have any. Check the freezer to be sure, though, cause I would like some."

Ember finally emerged from the back rooms. "There's no ice."

It was pretty obvious that she didn't want me rummaging through her kitchen as she walked to me and took the glass out of my hand, then gave it to Madison. "Here you go. I haven't had time to go shopping yet. I came straight home after having worked all night and crashed like a zombie."

Her hair was combed neatly and held back in a ponytail. She'd changed clothes, too, and was now wearing some jeans and a different t-shirt — this one free of holes. She'd ditched the old flip flops and was standing in her bare feet, hand on one hip as she turned to face me. "So, how long have you been contacting Madison without me knowing?"

"Since the day we came home, Mom," Madison answered her. "I got the phone number off that paper thingy I took from the resort. And after you left me at Gammy's and Gramp's, I called it and left my phone number and a message for Cohen to call me. And he did. Since then, we've talked a little bit now and then. I asked him if he wanted to come and see us since you were coming home today, and he said that he would love to."

Chewing on her lower lip, Ember leaned against the wall, her eyes on the floor. "And neither of you thought I might want to know about this before ambushing me in the school parking lot?"

I had to take the blame for that. "Ember, I wasn't thinking. I thought it would be a nice surprise, and I am sorry for doing that. You're right. I should've called you to ask if this was okay. But in all fairness, you didn't give me your number."

"You could've asked Madison for it." She went and sat across from her daughter. "Or you could've called me and asked, young lady. The thing I'm trying to get you both to understand is that I should've been asked."

"Well, you would've said no," Madison said with a frown. "And I wanted him to come. I missed him, Mom."

My heart sped up with the sweet sentiment. "I missed you both too." I took a seat at the table. "I'd like to take you girls out for dinner this evening. Madison, you can pick out any place you like."

"Well, I think Mom should pick it out since she's sort of mad at us." She looked at her mother. "You want to go somewhere that has shrimp? Or something else that you like but don't usually eat since I'm allergic to it?"

Madison's generous nature made her mother smile. Ember reached out and patted her on the back of the hand. "No, I don't want to eat anything like that. I think we should go to J.D. McDougal's." She looked at me. "You remember going to that place, Cohen?"

As if I could ever forget.

"Yeah, I remember going there, Ember. If I recall, there's an arcade there, and they serve some pretty tasty Italian food too. I think Maddy would enjoy it." I remembered how much Ember and I had enjoyed our date there. And after that date, we had gone back to my place and made love for the rest of the night. It wasn't close to this side of town, though. In fact, we hadn't gone out anywhere on the side of town we were from because we didn't want anyone we knew spotting us together.

I found it interesting that she'd brought up that specific place. That was the night that I'd done the only risky thing in our week together. She and I had made love quite a few times. And then I had this overwhelming urge to feel her without a condom on.

I'd managed to control myself, but she'd had an orgasm before I pulled out. That was the only time I felt that we could've made a baby. Even a few drops of semen was enough. Not that I had thought about it back then.

"Good!" Madison jumped up and clapped her hands. "I'm happy you guys are getting along now. When can we go?"

"It's about an hour from here." I looked at Ember to make sure she was on board. "Can we leave pretty soon?"

Nodding, she said, "We can leave soon. Madison, change your clothes first, though. I don't want you wearing your school uniform. And make sure you put it into the laundry basket in the bathroom, please."

"I will, Momma! Woohoo! I'm going to an arcade." Before she ran off, she looked at me with a beaming smile. "You make things fun. I'm glad you're here."

"Me too, sweetie."

As soon as she was out of sight, Ember asked, "Why'd you come here, Cohen?"

"To see you two."

She shook her head. "The real reason. Did you come here to talk me into taking your offer?"

"And if I did?"

"My mother and sister don't want me to take it."

"Let me guess." I was sure I knew why they were discouraging her. "They think my intentions are purely sexual, don't they?"

153

"Yep." She laughed. "I know you'd like things to go in that direction, too. But I know that's not the only reason you want me there."

"I've got more than one reason for wanting you there, Ember." We had a few minutes alone, and I wanted to use the time wisely. "I can make your lives a whole lot better. But I know leaving your family isn't an easy decision to make."

I just hope that if we share a child, you'll decide that I'm as much a part of your family as they are.

CHAPTER 24
EMBER

"I'm glad you understand, Cohen." His understanding didn't make my decision any easier, though.

Taking his wallet out of his back pocket, he pulled something out of it, then handed it to me. "This is a picture of my mother when she was a little girl. My brother, Baldwyn, got it off some ancestor website. We lost all the pictures in the fire. I guess I never looked at any of my parent's old pictures when I was a kid. I never knew what my mother looked like when she was that young."

A knot formed in my throat as I looked at the picture of a young girl — a girl who looked around Madison's age. Even though it was black and white, her resemblance with my child was unmistakable.

My hand shook as I placed the picture on the table. Cohen took it, putting it back into his wallet. He wouldn't take his eyes off me, and I knew exactly why. "My mother also had shellfish allergies, as did her maternal grandmother. My brother said that she used to say the allergy seemed to skip a generation."

He's figured it out.

He knew that I had lied to him for seven years. He knew that I'd had the chance to tell him about our daughter only two weeks ago and hadn't done it. He knew that I was a horrible person.

I'd been an awful bitch to him thus far. Screaming at him in public was the latest bitchy thing I'd done. It was time for me to stop acting that way toward a man who'd done nothing wrong.

Taking a deep breath, I finally said the only thing I could think of, "Cohen, I'm so sorry."

"Don't." He put his hand over mine, looking deep into my eyes.

"If they find out, Cohen…"

He stopped me. "Ember, we've got to do what's best for Madison. The adults will learn to accept things."

"You don't seem mad about this." I could barely breathe as my instincts told me to hang onto my hat — shit was about to get real.

"I'm not mad at you. I know how guilty you felt about telling your family about us. And I've done lots of thinking about how afraid you must've been back then when you found out that you were pregnant. I know you've been lying to everyone. And I know why you felt that you had to do it."

My stomach rumbled, and I felt like I was about to be sick. "Cohen, I'll be right back." I got up and ran to the bathroom, where I abruptly threw up.

Slowly, I slid to my knees, then into a sitting position as my mind spun out of control. My life seemed as if it was passing before my eyes, leaving no time for a single thought to take form in my brain.

Life as I had known it was about to change drastically. But not just for me — for my daughter, too. *What's she going to think of me?*

Having no idea what I was supposed to do next, I just sat there, hoping the answer would somehow come to me. There had to be an answer.

Suddenly, a knock on the door made my head turn slowly. "Yeah?"

"Ember, are you okay in there?" came Cohen's calm voice.

I couldn't figure out how he could be so calm about this. I had lied to the man. I had hidden his one and only child from him for her entire life. He had to be mad at me for doing that — no matter what he said. "Not really. I'm gonna stay in here for a bit in case I get sick again. Sorry about this." I rested my head against the cold porcelain toilet seat. "I'm sorry about everything, Cohen."

"It's okay. Just come out whenever you're ready."

I listened to his receding footsteps as he walked away. Tears filled my eyes — I knew I'd made so many huge mistakes in my life. And now, those mistakes were about to come to the surface for all to see.

With all the things I'd done to hurt Cohen and Madison, I knew it was finally the time to face the music. No matter how many people were mad at me. No matter how many people were disappointed in me. No matter how bruised and beaten my ego would get afterward — I had to tell everyone the truth.

How am I supposed to do that?

Even with the best of intentions, I knew how often I'd had chances of telling my family the truth, but, instead, I had chosen the easier path by lying.

When Madison was very little, not even a year old yet, she had a high fever, and we rushed her to the emergency room. Ashe had helped me to fill out the paperwork. When I had gotten to the section asking for the father's information, I had hesitated. She'd asked me if I was thinking about letting the father know about Madison.

She'd been right. With Madison being so sick, I had been thinking that I needed to let Cohen know about his child. Since it was Ashe who was with me then, I didn't tell the truth. I just told her that I was freaking out.

Ashe had asked me who the father was, and I told her that

she didn't know him and that I'd met him at a club. He was from out of town, and all I knew was his first name. I'd said that he'd told me his name was John and that I didn't think that was even his real name. I had then added that I was pretty sure he was married because he had a white spot around his ring finger in place of a wedding ring.

God, I am such a liar.

"Mom, what are you doing in there?" Madison asked through the keyhole of the locked door. "I'm ready to go. Are you fixing your hair and putting on makeup?"

"No." Putting my hands over my face, I knew it was nearly time to admit to my child that I was nothing more than a damn liar.

"Well, can you hurry up then so we can leave?"

"Sure." I got up then went to wash my face. I couldn't even look at myself in the mirror.

What made me so angry at myself was that I had never seen this day coming. Somehow, I had deceived myself to the point that I had thought I would never have to tell anyone the truth.

Finally, I looked at my reflection. "You are a fucking moron," I whispered as I glared at myself. "You make me sick."

Looking away, I felt another wave of nausea and turned just in time to puke into the toilet again. Tears rolled down my cheeks from the embarrassment I felt at my actions.

Another knock on the door. This time I knew I had to face him. Hiding in the bathroom for the rest of my life wasn't an option. I would just have to learn how to live with the shame. I would have to learn to deal with people knowing the truth about me.

"I'll be out in a minute."

"I'd like to talk to you."

"I need to brush my teeth." I didn't want to see him yet.

"It's going to be okay, baby. I promise you that it will all be okay."

I didn't deserve his kind words after how I'd done him so very wrong. But I had to stop thinking only about myself. "I'm going to brush my teeth, then I'll be out, and we can go."

"K."

No matter how much self-loathing I felt, I had to pull myself together. There was Madison to think about, and I couldn't show her this side of myself.

Somehow, I would have to stand tall even though I'd done some real damage to the people I loved. And I'd stolen years from my daughter and her father.

I couldn't make things about myself anymore. No matter what I'd told myself about why the lies were necessary to somehow protect everyone I cared about. I had to change the way I thought.

Honesty.

I would have to keep the word at the forefront of my mind from now on. It didn't matter if someone might get mad at me for being honest. I would just have to deal with that.

It hadn't even occurred to me how much I didn't want people to be mad at me. And yet, now that Cohen had every right to be furious with me, he wasn't mad at all. Or at least he was making me think he wasn't.

What if he's got something ruthless up his sleeve to get back at me?

Brushing my teeth, I tried not to think the worst about Cohen and his motives. Not everyone was as deceitful as I was. Not everyone was busily preparing lies and omissions to keep their asses covered at all times.

As soon as I came out of the bathroom, I saw Cohen leaning against the wall with his hands in his pockets. "Maddy asked me if it would be okay for her to take her friend who lives next door with us. I told her it would be fine. She ran over to get her."

"K." It wasn't as if I cared if Maddy brought her friend, Kylie.

Just as I turned to go to my bedroom to get my purse, I felt his hand on my arm. "Hey, I don't want you to kick yourself over this."

A short laugh burst out of me. "Easy for you to say. You haven't been lying to everyone you care about for nearly a decade. Very soon, everyone I love will know that I'm nothing but a liar."

"You don't have to tell everyone at once. Right now, it's enough for me to know she's mine. We'll wait to tell Madison until we think the time is right. And we can wait even longer to tell your family if that's what you want to do. I'm not trying to turn your world upside down. I just want to start working out how we're going to do what's best for our daughter."

"Our daughter," I echoed. "I've never heard anyone say that about her – I've always considered her just mine." Looking into his eyes, I had to admit something to him. "You know, it's nice to hear it. It's nice to know that I'm not alone in this parenting thing anymore."

"This might sound odd coming from me, but I'm extremely happy that you were so quick to let me know she's mine. I had my fears that you might try to hide it. I'm over the moon that Madison is my daughter. Our daughter."

I felt a little bit of the tension fall off my shoulders. "I am so happy to hear you say that. You've got no idea how happy that makes me. Cohen, I would really like to put my lying years behind me. The weight of the deceit is oppressive. And even with just you knowing the truth now, I have to say that I feel a tiny bit lighter. If I can figure out how to stop all my self-loathing, I feel like I might just make it through this."

"You're gonna make it through this." He pulled me into his arms, hugging me tightly. "I'm gonna make sure of that."

My arms wrapped around him as I buried my face in his broad chest. "Oh my God, this feels so good. You have no idea."

"I've got some idea." He kissed the top of my head. "You feel like home in my arms. You always did."

Pulling my head off of his chest, I looked up at him to find him smiling. "With all that I've done to hurt you, do you honestly think you'll be able to get past this?"

"I already have. I know why you did the things you've done. I'm not judging you for it either. I can't say what I would've done had you told me the truth back then. So, I'm not going to hold you accountable for the last seven years."

"What about the last couple of weeks?"

He shook his head. "What matters is that you're being honest with me now. That's all that matters, baby."

Although I loved it when he called me baby, I knew we had to do everything we could to slowly ease into this new situation with our daughter. "Let's try to figure out how to do this right, so we don't scar our kid. Agreed?"

"Agreed."

At least we can agree on things that affect our child. I hope we can agree on the things that affect our relationship, too.

CHAPTER 25
COHEN

Ember wasn't exactly back to being her old self, but she wasn't acting as distant as she'd been recently. Sipping on red wine as she looked at the menu, she seemed a lot more relaxed. "I'm thinking about ordering the lobster ravioli." Peering over the top of the large menu, she asked, "What about you? What do you think you're gonna get?"

"Why?" I teased her, knowing she wanted me to get something that she might want to try too. She'd done that every time we'd eaten out before.

"Well, I could share my ravioli with you, and you could share — oh, let's say the chicken parmigiana with me — if you got that." Putting the menu down, she looked around for the girls and saw them playing air hockey. "And the girls will take a pizza. Cheese, as usual."

It wasn't like I cared what I ate anyway. "The chicken parm sounds good to me." Putting my menu away, I knew I needed to broach the subject of them moving to Austin. As much as I didn't want to rush her, I couldn't stop myself. "Ember, I don't want you to go back to that job."

Her eyelashes fluttered as she nodded. "I guessed as much."

"There're a few ways we could handle this. I could just give you money so you wouldn't have to work to pay the bills. But that's not what I really want to do." I wanted my family under one roof. But I knew that would really be rushing things.

"I know. You want us to come to Austin." She sighed as she looked into my eyes. "I'm sorry. I really am, Cohen. Facing the fact that I'm not the person I've been telling myself that I am isn't easy. Until I saw you again, it had been years since I thought of myself as a big fat liar. Sure, in the very beginning, telling lies wasn't so easy. But after Madison's first birthday, my family stopped bringing up her father altogether, so it was easier to just forget everything."

"Until you saw me." I understood her completely. But it was now her turn to try to understand me. "Ember, I forgive you for keeping this from me. But you need to consider *my* feelings now. Your parents and sister have been there for you and Madison this whole time. I get that you want to consider their feelings in all this. But *I'm* here now. You won't need to depend on them for a thing, as far as our daughter is concerned."

"You're saying that I need to make you and Madison my first priorities." She sipped some more wine as she took that in.

"I think you've always made Madison your first priority." I didn't want her to think I was accusing her of neglecting our daughter – because I wasn't. "And I haven't been in the picture for you to think about anyway. I just want you to add me in there, right behind our daughter. I've missed out on so much already — I don't want to miss out on anything else. You understand, don't you?"

"How could I not understand?" Her eyes turned up to the ceiling, and I sensed that she was fighting a battle inside herself. "I know that asking you for more time would be an insult. So, I won't ask." Her eyes moved to mine. "But can you think about us keeping this a secret from my family for a while? Just until we straighten out some things. And only because this is making me physically sick, Cohen. You heard me barfing my guts out after you found out the truth. I've been lying right to their faces for years. And I'll have to face Ashe when I tell her that I had sex with her ex, too. I might pass out. I might have a heart attack and die of shame."

It would've been nice if Ember didn't feel so ashamed of being with me. "You know, Ember, I'm considered to be quite the catch. I'm sure you could do worse."

"Well, now, yeah — for sure." She shook her head. "But back then, you had one hell of a bad reputation. You know, I bet you can't count how many women you've been with since your first sexual experience, Cohen."

This wasn't where I wanted our conversation to head. Luckily, the waitress showed up. "Are you ready to order?"

Ember nodded, then I gave her our order. "She'll have the lobster ravioli. I'll have the chicken parmigiana. And the kids will share a medium cheese pizza."

"What type of noodles would you like for the chicken parmigiana, sir?"

I looked at Ember. "Honey?"

"Linguini," Ember said with a smile.

This was the old Ember, the girl I couldn't get enough of. She had just enough of a take-charge attitude, mixed with a giving nature, sprinkled with the ability to make me happier than anyone ever had. And her smile could make my heart skip a beat. "Linguini it is."

"I'll have this out to you soon."

"I'm glad you know now," Ember whispered. "I don't have to be on guard with you anymore. I didn't like keeping you at a distance. I like being with you in this way. This feels so natural — the other way felt like hell."

"To me, too." There were a few more hurdles we had to make it through, but we'd get there. "I think we can use my family as a test run for how to handle yours when it comes to telling them about our daughter and us. We can tell my brothers about this together and see how it goes. It might help you when the time comes to tell your family."

Pursing her lips, she seemed to be considering my plan. "Hmm. I think you believe that having me with you when you tell them will make it much harder for them to pressure you into doing things you might not want. Such as getting a paternity test done. And maybe things like making legal agreements for me to sign, saying I can't have any of your money. And maybe even a custody agreement that's legally binding."

With a chuckle, I had to hand it to her. "Yeah, you caught me."

"See, it's not so easy to just tell your family about this and to expect only congratulations from them." Her lips turned down into a frown. "All of them have every right to think the worst of me. I've lied and hidden things from you for seven long years. And then when I actually had a chance to tell you the truth, I ran away, leaving you with no information on how to contact me again."

"Stop doing that to yourself." I hated that she was beating herself up over the past. "You know that you did everything in Madison's best interest."

Picking up her glass of wine, she took a long drink instead of the sips she'd been taking, then put it down in front of her. Her eyes and hand fixed on the remainder of the wine left in the glass, I watched her as she gulped it down. "That's not true."

"Of course, it's true."

"Cohen, you need to know the whole truth." Her eyes came to mine as she took a deep breath. "Once I saw you at the resort, I went into another mode. Not that of a mother, but a woman who desperately doesn't want to be uncovered for being a huge liar. Since seeing you again, everything I've done was for selfish reasons – I was trying to cover my own ass."

I found that impossible to believe. "Come on, Ember.

That's not the person I knew back then. Madison had to be at the heart of what you did. You must've been afraid that I might take you to court and get custody of her. That had to be floating around in your head somewhere. You just don't want to tell me that. You're afraid that if I haven't thought of that yet, I will now."

"No." She shook her head. "It's all been purely selfish. I swear that to you. If it wasn't about keeping my lie, then it was about keeping my distance from you – staying away from the temptation you represent." She took another deep breath as if that had been challenging for her to admit it aloud. "But there has been tremendous guilt over keeping you and Madison apart since I saw you again. There is that. But I wasn't going to tell you about her — I wanted to save myself the shame and embarrassment of being found out as a fraud."

I wasn't sure what to think. Sitting back, I stared at her. Almost a decade had gone by without us seeing each other. I had to admit to myself that I didn't really know the person she'd become.

I really can't rush into a relationship with this woman.

"You know, I'm sure there are lots of things we have to learn about each other. We don't have to rush a thing." That wasn't entirely true. "Well, we don't have to rush anything other than making this family legit. I will want my name on her birth certificate. I'm assuming the father's information was left blank."

"It is blank." Inhaling, she seemed to be trying to gather herself to talk about our daughter and what would be best for her. "I'd like to tell Madison about this before we take that step."

"That step has to be taken either way, Ember. I can have my lawyer handle it as soon as tomorrow. It'll take time for a new birth certificate to come in, anyway. And when we enroll her in school in Austin, I want her enrolled as Madison Nash. You can see how that needs to be taken care of ASAP." It was time Ember learned who I'd become. I'd been in charge of overseeing every branch of our resort, which meant I'd become extremely good at making things happen — and fast.

Her face turned pale, and she closed her eyes. "God, this is really happening, isn't it?" she whispered.

I didn't want her to get sick over this. But I couldn't let her slow down the process of making Madison my legal daughter either. "Baby, you've gotta just breathe and know that I'm not going to hurt you or our daughter. I just want to make sure she'll always be provided for, and that includes making sure I'm her legal father. You're going to have to trust me. I want what's best for all of us. I'd love it if you could want that now too."

"All of us?" The color started returning to her face, making her cheeks flush. "That sounds pretty amazing to me." Cocking her head to one side, she asked, "Do you honestly think you can get past all I've done?"

Reaching across the table, I placed my hand over hers. "Ember, all I want to do is get on with the here and now. We can let the past go so that we embrace our future. We have a future as a family — the three of us."

At least I hope we do.

CHAPTER 26
EMBER

I'd agreed with Cohen on everything. He'd gotten me the job in security at the resort. I would work the morning shift in the safety deposit room from eight a.m. to four p.m. Monday through Friday. All weekends and holidays off, two weeks of paid vacation each year, and all the insurances imaginable. All those perks made the job too good to pass up.

After staying one night in Houston, he rushed back to Austin to put things in motion. His lawyer had already gotten the paperwork needed to add him to Madison's birth certificate and change her last name to Nash.

I had one week to sell the things I didn't want to take with us and pack the rest. I was getting rid of more than what I was taking.

As of yet, Madison only knew that we'd be moving to Austin so I could take a job at the resort and that we'd be living in Cohen's guesthouse. And she was over the moon about it.

Madison was busy going through her box of toys and sorting through them. "Mom, I think I'm too old for this one." She came into the kitchen, where I was packing the dishes into a box. Before I could comment on the baby rattle she was holding in her hand, she asked, "You're taking those to the new house?"

"No." Cohen had told me the house was completely furnished, so I didn't need to take a stick of furniture. Plus, the kitchen was completely equipped with all we'd need, so I wasn't to take anything from my kitchen either. "I'm packing them up because I've got someone coming over to pick them up soon. I've pretty much sold everything that we don't need. All I've got to do is wait for people to show up, hand me cash, then take this stuff away."

"Even my bed?"

"Even your bed." I noticed the way her jaw hung open, and I figured I'd better clear things up for her. "You and I won't be staying here anymore. Cohen got us a room at a hotel about a mile from here. It's the one he stayed in last night. He said you'll love the pool. We'll come back here each day until we've got everything sold and gone or packed and ready."

"Oh." Nodding, she seemed to agree with the plan. "That sounds fun. Like another vacation. He's so nice to us, Momma."

"Yes, he's very nice to us." I pointed at the rattle she was holding. "And yes, you have outgrown that. Put it in the box of toys that I'm going to donate to the second-hand shop."

"K." She ran off, disappearing down the hallway.

I was back to work, packing the dishes when my cell rang. I'd given Cohen my number and had gotten his before he left. His name glowed on the screen.

Smiling, I answered, "You miss me already?"

"Maddy must not be around," he said with a soft chuckle, "or you wouldn't be so flirty with me."

"She's in her room sorting through her toybox." Now that he knew the truth, the natural attraction I had for him had bubbled up to the surface, begging to be let out. "To what do I owe the pleasure of your call?"

"I've found a private school that I think we should consider for Madison. I'm about to text you a link to the website so you can look it over. Feel free to call them if you like. Ask all the questions a parent needs to ask. It's not like I have a clue about that sort of thing."

"Like I do." I hadn't been able to afford anything other than public school. "She's only been in two schools in the last two years, and both of those have been public ones. Maybe your brother Baldwyn could help you figure out what to ask."

"Ours is the only one in school, babe."

I found that kind of funny. "You're the second youngest, and you've got the oldest kid." I had to laugh. "You got started earlier than any of them."

"Yes, *we* did." He wasn't going to let me off the hook about my part in making our daughter. "You do recall how you wouldn't let me go that one time we went at it without coverage, right?"

"Damn. You remembered that, did ya?"

"Vividly."

My thighs got hot just talking about it. "What can I say? It felt extremely good."

"I know we haven't agreed to officially date yet. But do us both a favor and get on some birth control so when we do get back to what we do best, we can do it without my cock being covered."

There was more to think about than just pregnancy. "I will do that this very afternoon. But I want you to go see a doctor too."

"For what?"

"To check for anything you might've picked up from the many, many sexual partners you've had in the last seven years." I wasn't going to be having sex with that man until he was cleared by a doctor and some thorough lab work.

"Damn, baby," he sounded a little embarrassed.

"I've gotta protect myself." I finished with the kitchen stuff and closed the box.

"Well, you make sure the doctor checks you for STDs too," he said smartly.

"Cohen, *you* were my last sexual partner."

"Are you sure about that?"

"Absolutely. I know I've lied, but not about that." I took a seat on the sofa, taking a break for a moment.

"You've gotta stop, baby. You're making me hot for you. I don't know how long I can wait. I know you'll be here in a week, but I'm thinking I might have to use the company jet to get back to you tonight."

"Slow your roll. We've still got to take things slow." Twirling a lock of my hair around my finger, I liked thinking about how hot I could actually make him — when the time came. And I knew it would come. "We'll be there in a week. But we still can't be together like that right off the bat. It's going to take time. There's already going to be so much for her to take in. She's our top priority."

"You act like she never sleeps." He laughed to let me know he was just kidding around.

"Ha, ha." Another call came in, and this one was from my sister. "It's Ashe, Cohen. Let me take the call, then I'll call you back."

"K. And I do miss you already."

"Me too. Bye." I couldn't wipe the smile off of my face as I answered her call. "Hi, sis."

"I'm about to pull up and thought I'd call to let you know. I saw your post on that city-wide garage sell site and had to wonder what the hell you're doing."

"Good. I've got some big news. I'll fill you in when you get here." I'd been waiting until I could tell her in person, and it seemed that the time had come.

I thought it would be best if Madison didn't witness her aunt saying nasty things about Cohen or overhearing anything we said. "Madison, can you come here?"

Running into the living room, she asked, "Yeah, Mom?"

"Can you go next door and play with Kylie for a little bit? Aunt Ashe is about to arrive, and we've got grownup things to talk about."

"She's gonna be mad about us moving, isn't she?"

"Probably. And you know how I don't like you to hear curse words. So, scat, will ya?" I got up and went to the door. Pulling it open, I saw my sister getting out of her car. "Hurry."

Madison rushed out of the house and then knocked on the door right next to ours. Kylie's mom opened the door. "Can I come in and play with Kylie for a little while?"

"Sure, Madison." Beth looked at me then at my sister. "She'll be fine over here, Ember. You guys visit."

I'd already informed Beth about our move. We'd been friends since I'd moved in, so she knew there was going to be tension between me and my sister when I raised the issue. "Thanks."

"So, tell me, what is this all about, Ember?" Ashe walked into the apartment, eyeing everything and finding boxes all over the place. "You look like you're getting rid of everything."

Closing the door, I prepared myself for a fight. "Yeah, I am getting rid of the majority of our things. I've got a new job. I start next Monday."

Confusion riddled her face. "So, you're moving?"

"Yeah. It's a bit too far to commute," I joked.

"Have you told your company that you've taken another job?"

"I told my boss this morning." I took a seat on the couch. "Have a seat, sis."

"I'd rather stand. I've got a feeling that I'm going to have to give you a lecture very soon."

I knew she would try. But it wouldn't change my mind. "All I have to say is that it would be selfish of you to try to change my mind. This job will make it so I can actually raise my own kid. It's at the resort we went to in Austin."

Her jaw dropped. "Cohen's resort?"

"The one he and his brothers own, yes." I prepared myself to hear her say terrible things about the man I was pretty sure I was falling in love with.

"So, you two have been talking since you left the resort. I see." She held her jaw firm, her lips forming a thin line. "You know the kind of man he is, and yet you've been talking to him behind my back."

That threw me off. "Behind your back? I wasn't aware you still spoke to him," I said sarcastically. "Look, Ashe. I know what you think of him. But he's not that way anymore," I defended him.

"Have you seen his social media pages, Ember? He's got more girls on there than men. And there are lots of pictures of him partying it up with girls all over him."

I didn't want to see any of that. I made a mental note to ask him to please get off social media for my sake and our daughter's or remove some of those pictures at least. Madison didn't need to stumble across anything like that. "I don't want to talk about that. I just want to finally be honest with you about things."

Her knees seemed to buckle, and she sat down heavily next to me on the sofa. "You need to be *honest* with me — *finally*? What have you been so far, Ember?"

"A liar," I confessed. I was done being afraid of what my family would think of me. I had to put my shame behind me, or I wouldn't ever be able to move forward.

Three lines formed on her forehead. "What have you lied about?"

"Seven years ago, I spent one week with Cohen Nash."
She gulped. "Why?"

"Because we ran into each other in the mall, and there was this spark between us that neither of us could ignore." I didn't want to hurt her, but she needed to know that I hadn't betrayed her for something that wasn't special. "We had the most amazing week, Ashe. But then guilt over what I was doing to you got to me, and I ended things with him."

A stunned expression took over where confusion had been. "*You* broke up with *him?*"

"For you, I did. I didn't want what we had to end, but I knew it would hurt you, so I broke things off. And two months later, I took a pregnancy test and found out that we'd made a baby during that magical week."

Her chest caved in as she completely deflated. "You've hidden this from all of him and us for *seven* years?"

"I have. But now he knows. And we're going to tell Madison sometime after she and I move into his guesthouse. If things go the way I think — actually, hope is a better word — then he and I will start seeing each other again."

"I see." She looked like a train had hit her.

I reached out, touching her shoulder. "Ashe, I didn't do any of this to hurt you. But I think he and I are falling in love. At least, I know that I am."

Her eyes met mine as she seemed to be trying to understand and make some sense out of everything I'd told her. "You *love* him?"

"Yeah, I think that I do. And I think we've got a real shot at making a family for our daughter – and also for ourselves. Please, don't try to get in the way of Madison having a real family, Ashe. I know you love her and want what's best for her."

"I want what's best for you both, Ember." A tear ran down her cheek. "I wish you all the best, sister." She wrapped her arms around me, and I hugged her back, shocked.

Well, that didn't go anywhere near how I'd thought it would. Thank God.

I'd never been so nervous in my entire life. Butterflies swarmed inside my stomach as I drove up to my home. A home I would now share with my daughter and her mother.

Although they weren't going to live in the house yet – the plan was for them to start off in the guesthouse while we all got used to things — I hoped it wouldn't take long for things to change. I wanted us all under one roof. I wanted us to become the kind of family Madison deserved.

Ember had called to tell me that they were there, but I didn't have to rush home or anything as they would still be settling in. And that's when I went to my oldest brother's office.

Baldwyn didn't know about my visit to Houston the week before. I hadn't told a soul about it. But the time had come to let him in on things. "Hey, big brother."

"Hey, Cohen. What's up?" He got up from behind his desk and went to sit on the loveseat, gesturing to the couch. "Have a seat."

As I sat down, I felt like I might be in for a fight. "So, I went to see Ember, and she told me the truth about Madison."

Lines formed on his forehead. "Or you think she's told you the truth."

"No, I know it's the truth. I'm a father, Baldwyn."

His eyes on the floor, he huffed. "I want you to get a paternity test done before you do anything else."

"I've already been added to her birth certificate as her father." I held my jaw tight as I waited for his reaction to my news.

Slowly, he pulled his head up until our eyes met. "You did what?"

"I'm officially her father now. And her last name is Nash. I want it that way. I didn't need some stupid test to tell me what I feel in my soul — she is my child. I know she is."

"Well, Cohen, if you won't follow my suggestion about that, then please follow my suggestion about getting some agreements between you and her mother done in a legal fashion." He got up and started pacing back and forth, clearly upset by my news. "If you don't have something iron-clad about custody, then she could try to take your kid away from you again. And you can't have that happening." He stopped pacing and looked at me with a stern expression. "For your child's sake, Cohen."

"I don't think I need to go that route. Ember and I are in agreement about the way we want to raise our daughter. They're moving into my guesthouse today. Ember is going to be working here, at the resort. And we've enrolled Madison in a private school here. She starts Monday, and she can't wait."

Shaking his head, he still wasn't convinced that I was doing things in the best way. "You need legal documents to keep things safe. You need to keep your daughter and your money safe."

"I know that if things don't work out between Ember and me, then I can expect her to ask for child support. But I don't think it'll come to that. But, if it does, then I'll deal with it at the time." He had no idea how much I didn't want to cloud things with lawyers and trips to the courthouse. "Baldwyn, I think I'm in love with Ember. With time and patience, I think she and I can build the family our daughter needs and deserves. Making Ember sign things about money and custody look like they will get in the way of what I really want with her."

"But you have more important things to worry about than what *might* happen between you two. You just need to cover your ass." He didn't seem like he was going to let this go.

"I know you're only thinking about what's best for me."

"And your daughter, Cohen. I'm not saying this for any other reason than to make sure her mother can't take her away from you and deprive you of more years with her. You have to understand that your feelings for Ember might be getting in the way of you making good decisions for yourself and your daughter."

"Baldwyn, you know I love you and respect the hell out of you too. But I cannot bring myself to think like that. I have to show Ember that I trust her. After all she's done, after all she's been through, I have to show her that she is trustworthy."

"But she's not," he reminded me. "She's proven herself not to be trustworthy at all. She didn't come to you to tell you about your daughter. You went to her."

I knew I wouldn't get him to see things my way, and I had to be okay with that. "We're going to have to agree to disagree. And I fully expect you to treat Ember with respect. I know her. I know the woman she was before all this happened. And with some trust and love, I know she'll thrive. Without that trust and love, that girl I first fell in love with won't be able to come back to me. And I want her back — completely."

"Good luck with that. You have my word, Cohen. I won't treat her bad in any way. All of us should get together soon to welcome your daughter into our family."

"That's what I like to hear, brother."

With things settled between us, I'd taken off to get home. That's when the butterflies began. But Baldwyn's words kept running through my head throughout the whole way home.

What if he's right and I'm wrong?

Parking my truck in the garage, I knew I had to think only positive thoughts. I made my way through the house, then out the patio door in the back. Stopping just as I got out on the patio, I took a deep breath.

They're here, and that's all that matters.

The door to the guesthouse flew open before I got all the way to the guesthouse, and Madison came running out. "This is so beautiful!" She jumped into my arms, and we hugged. "I'm so glad you're letting us live here!"

"I'm so glad you want to live here." I looked at Ember, who couldn't seem to wipe the smile off her face. "I'm so glad you came."

"This place is insane, Cohen." She walked up to us. "It's a lot to take in. But we love everything about the guesthouse."

"Yeah, it's the best house I've ever lived in," Madison said as I put her back on her feet.

"You guys want a tour of the main house?" That was where I really wanted them to be. Not that I was going to rush them. But I felt like if they knew what lay just across the patio from them, they might want to join me sooner rather than later.

"Cohen, if you show her what's in there, she's not going to be as happy with the guesthouse," Ember warned me. "Might wanna wait on that for a bit."

Madison only shook her head. "I'm always gonna be happy with the guesthouse, Momma."

I knew Ember was right, though, and so I took Madison by the hand. "Well, take me into your new house and show me where you're gonna be sleeping."

Madison's lower lip jutted out as she looked at the open patio door that led into my house. "Really?"

Shrugging, I looked at Ember for that answer. "I really would love to show it to you guys."

"Oh, okay, fine, let's go take a tour of his mansion." Ember followed along as I led them inside.

"This isn't a mansion," I began the tour as we walked inside. "Now, my brothers have mansions, so when we go visit them, you'll find out what is the difference. And one of my brothers and his family lives in Ireland, and they own a castle."

"A castle?" Madison's eyes narrowed as if she didn't entirely believe me.

"Yes, a castle," I said. "A real one with a moat and a drawbridge and everything. I'll have to take you there to see it very soon."

"Cohen," Ember cautioned me. "Let's not overwhelm her."

"You're right. First things first. This is the kitchen where my younger brother sometimes comes over and cooks for me," I walked them through the space. "He's a chef."

"Wow," Madison was impressed. "This is really big, and it looks like something out of a movie."

I kept moving, showing them one room after another until we ended back in the living room. "And there you have it — the grand tour. So, do you still love the guesthouse, Maddy?"

"I do still love it. I love all of this. And I love that we get to live close to you." She looked at her mother. "Aren't you glad too, Momma?"

"I am overjoyed." Ember took a seat then patted the place next to her on the sofa. "Come here, Madison." She looked at me. "Cohen, will you take a place on her other side?" There was a look in her golden-brown eyes that surprised me.

I wasn't one hundred percent positive, but it seemed as if Ember was ready to tell Madison the truth. Taking a deep breath, I took the seat on the other side of our daughter and waited to see what was coming next. My heart was barely beating, and I had no idea what was about to happen.

"Momma, why are you looking at Cohen that way?" After we'd locked eyes, Madison started looking back and forth between her mother and me. "And why are you looking at Mom like that, Cohen?"

Ember gave me a nod, and I couldn't believe it. "You sure?"

"I am," she confirmed.

"You guys are freaking me out," Maddy informed us.

I didn't want to freak her out, so I looked into her eyes and took her hands into mine. "Madison Michelle, so many things are about to change for you. All of them for the better. You're getting a new home, a new school, and you and I are both getting something super special."

Her eyes shimmered with excitement. "Like what?"

Ember put her hand on Maddy's shoulder, drawing her attention away from me. "Honey, I know we haven't talked about your father much. And I know that this might come as a shock to you. See, I knew Cohen seven years ago, after he dated your Aunt Ashe. The fact is we fell in love, and then we got separated by life for some time. He didn't know something very important. Not until last week when he came to visit us."

She looked back at me. "What did you find out when you came to visit us?"

"Before I tell you about that, let me tell you that I have loved your mother for all seven years we were apart. And I still do."

"Good!" Madison laughed. "I think you are the perfect couple. I see hearts in both your eyes when you look at each other."

I looked into my daughter's eyes. "What do you see in mine right now?"

She looked a little confused as she stared deep into my eyes. "I think I see hearts for me."

"You do see hearts for you," I let her know. "You see them because I love you. And not just because you're the best kid in the world either. See, Madison, your mother gave me a gift way back then that I didn't know about until last week."

"What was it?" she asked with wide eyes.

"It was *you*, sweetie. *You* are *my* little girl." I looked at Ember, who had rivers rolling down her red cheeks. "You are *our* little girl, Madison Michelle Nash. I'm your dad."

Tears filled her eyes, and at the same time, mine grew blurry, and we all held each other and cried.

My heart has never been so full.

Our first family hug proved to be even more emotional than I'd imagined. The tears on all of our faces told me that every single one of us was happier than we'd ever been.

The lies are finally behind me.

I'd been the one pushing not to rush things, but once we were all together and seeing so much love in Cohen's eyes, I knew it was time to set the truth free to our daughter. She deserved to get to start things knowing that she had a father who loved her.

Cohen got up, leaving us in the living room, and then returned with a box of tissues. "I had to search pretty hard to find these, but here you go, girls."

I pulled out a handful of tissues and dabbed Madison's eyes before my own. "Here you go, sweetie. I'll clean you up."

"Momma, what does all this mean?"

Cohen sat back down beside her. "It means that the three of us know about this, but we can't tell your grandparents or your aunt quite yet."

"Oh." I hadn't told Cohen the news yet. "I've been so busy with things that I forgot to tell you."

"Tell me what?"

"I've already told my family, Cohen. Ashe was surprisingly okay with it, and once my parents saw that, they didn't have much to say. Other than that, they wish us the best."

"See," Madison said smugly. "I told you Aunt Ashe wouldn't be mad about you liking Cohen." She grinned as she looked at Cohen. "I mean, Dad."

His hand went to his heart as his eyes grew shiny again. "Oh, my God. You have no idea what you've just done to me." He hugged her again, tears running down his cheeks as he looked at me. "I'm her *dad*. She called me *Dad*."

Madison laughed. "I didn't mean to make you cry again." She waited a second before adding, "Dad."

"Oh, my heart!" he wailed. "You've got it in the palm of your hand, little girl. *My* little girl."

He finally let her go and grabbed the box of tissues, blowing his nose and wiping his eyes. "I can't remember the last time I cried. I was just a kid, I think."

"No more crying," Madison declared. "I've got something I want to say."

"Go ahead, honey," I said as I beamed at her. "Say whatever you want. Ask us anything you want. We'll tell you the truth." I was over the moon that I didn't have to hide anything anymore. It made my heart ache and made me want to keep on telling more and more truths.

"Well, I would like to ask if we can live in here with you, Dad, instead of out back there."

I wagged my finger at Cohen. "I told you that if you showed her this house, she wouldn't be happy with the other one."

"It's not that, Mom," Madison corrected me. "It's just that I want us to start being a real family right away. I want to see my daddy when I wake up and go to sleep, and I want to eat breakfast and dinner with him. And I want that with you too, Mom. I don't want us to live in different houses."

Cohen smiled as he nodded. "Of course, you can live in

here with me. I've wanted that from the moment I saw your mother again."

Once again, I was reminded that he'd wanted me before he even had a clue that we shared a child. "Really?"

"Really." Jerking his thumb back, he told Madison, "So come on back and show me which one of the bedrooms you want."

Jumping up, she took off like a flash with him right at her heels. "I know just the one!"

Since they would be busy for a bit, I went back out to the guesthouse to get our suitcases, thankful that we hadn't unpacked them yet. Walking outside, I took a moment to take in the gorgeous swimming pool. The waterfall feature sparkled as the sun was setting behind it.

Life would be so very different than it had been. *Life will be so much better now.*

I felt light as air as I drifted towards the guesthouse like a weight had been magically lifted off my shoulders. From the moment we'd walked into the gorgeous home, Madison and I had been captivated by all the beautiful surroundings.

I'd been sure we would be happy as could be — just living in that house. But now we were moving in with Cohen. We were about to become something real and substantial. We were a family and would be living as such.

After picking up Madison's luggage, I went back into the house to see what they were up to. I found Madison sitting right next to her father as they looked at the laptop resting on his lap. "I like this." She pointed out something on the screen.

"Unicorns?" he asked. "You like those silly-looking horses?"

"I love them." Her eyes turned to me. "You got my clothes. Thanks, Mom. Me and Dad are picking out a new bedspread and curtains for my room."

"Can you show me which one you picked out so that I can unpack your things?"

"Yeah." She pointed at the computer screen again. "And some pink curtains can go with that. It'll look super cute."

"I'm thinking a plush pink rug might look super cute too," Cohen said as he wiggled his dark brows.

"Who knew you were such an avid decorator for little girls' bedrooms?" I laughed as I followed Madison down the hallway.

"You're gonna find out a lot about me that you didn't know, Ember Wilson," he called out after me.

I certainly hope so.

"I like this one right here." She walked through the door of the first bedroom on the right. There was a sitting room complete with a sofa and a loveseat, an enormous television on the wall, and that was only the beginning. From there, we went through another door and into the actual bedroom. A king-size bed took up a fair amount of space as it stood in the middle of the enormous room.

Everything matched, from the white-washed wood making up the bed's headboard and footboard to the three dressers sitting in front of three of the walls. The closet door was right across from the bed. Madison darted in front of me to open it. "In here, Mom."

Taking her things into the closet, I marveled at its size. "I can't believe there are washing machines and dryers in each walk-in closet." I placed the bags on the floor. "You know that you can't mess with those, right? And don't ever climb into them."

"Do you think I'm some kind of a crazy person, Momma?" She put her hands on her hips as she looked at me as if I were insane. "I'm not about to climb into a washer or a dryer. And I don't even know how to use them. So, you'll still have to do my clothes for me."

I began taking out the clothes, and she helped me put them where she could reach them. "I like how there's a low thingy for me to hang my clothes on. It's like he knew I was going to come and live here."

"It's really for pants. But I'm glad you like it." There was so much space that even with all her clothes put away, it still looked bare. "Man, I'm gonna have to buy you more clothes. It'll take us forever to fill this closet."

"And you'll have to get yourself more clothes too, Momma. You'll have a big closet like this one too. Which room are you gonna pick?"

"The one next to yours, of course." I wasn't going to stay too far from her. "That way, if you wake up and are afraid for any reason, then you can just come to my room."

"I could just call you on the phone and tell you to come. That's what I do at Grammy's since their bedroom and mine are on opposite sides of the house." Her eyes glassed over a little. "They can come to visit us here, right?"

"I'm sure they can." I wasn't sure Ashe would even want to come to see us at Cohen's home – she'd wished me well, but I wasn't sure she was ready for a front-row seat to my new life with her ex-boyfriend. I couldn't let that bother me, though. "We'll invite them over sometime soon."

"Yeah, we should." She led the way out of the room. "Let's go get your things and put them away. I'll help you."

"You're such a good little helper." I followed her back to the living room, where Cohen was sitting in a chair, tapping away at his computer. "You look like you've found plenty to order for her room."

"I have." He turned the screen around to show us what he'd gotten. "That room will soon look like a little girl's dream come true. If she has unicorn dreams."

"That's way too much," I moaned. He'd picked out so many things.

"No, it's not, Mom." Madison gave me a stern look. "I love unicorns, you know."

"I would have nightmares in a room with that much stuff."

I could already see that Cohen would spoil Madison rotten – and she'd enjoy every last second of it.

"Mom said she's gonna take the room right next to mine," Madison said as she climbed up on the chair to sit next to Cohen. "What do you think about that, Dad?"

"I think your mother can pick out whichever bedroom she wants." He looked at me. "This is your home."

I turned to leave. "You're being very generous. And don't think we don't appreciate it."

"You know, Kylie's mom and dad share a bedroom. And Grammy and Gramps do too," Madison said.

I kept walking. "Because they're married, honey."

"Married?" she sounded a little unsure of what that word meant. "Dad, are you and Mom married since you guys had me?"

I froze in place, unable to move. I wasn't sure how to answer that question.

Cohen was quick to say, "No. Not all people who have children together are married. That's not what being married means. When you find someone you love very, very much, you might decide that you want to live the rest of your life with them. And only then would you ask someone to marry you."

"Are you gonna ask Momma to marry you then?"

Good Lord, this child is going to embarrass me to death!

CHAPTER 29
COHEN

A month had passed since Madison and Ember had moved in with me. Seeing them every single day only made me happier each day that passed. I knew there would be no other way I would ever want to live.

The only thing that would've made it better was if Ember and I could get going with our relationship. We'd both been so set on making sure our daughter felt comfortable with the new situation that we hadn't taken any time for ourselves.

Ember had the new job to keep her busy, too. And Madison had the new school and daycare to adjust to. Since daycare was in the resort, she loved it – I couldn't help feeling a sense of pride that my baby girl loved the resort as much as I did.

All in all, there were so many changes that we had to get used to. And with all the settling in we had to do, Ember and I hadn't let romance come into play.

Yet.

Now that I had a daughter to think about, I knew I had to do things differently than I had done in the past. I had to show Madison how a man was supposed to treat a woman. I had to instill in her some ideas about what she should expect from men and how they treated her.

Me, being the kind of man I'd been – a real horn-dog – I needed to prepare her for a world full of those rascals. I needed to make sure that she knew what she was getting into if she ever hooked up with that type of guy.

So, I set out to do things in such a way that they would leave a mark on our daughter. A mark that would show her to never accept anything but the best from a guy who thought he had a chance in hell with her.

Ever since running into Ember again, we hadn't even shared one kiss. I'd treated her with the utmost respect – paying attention to her boundaries and not trying to push things. But now it was time to show her that I wanted romance. I had to do it in such a way that Madison would see that she too could only accept love when it was given to her in the appropriate way.

So I called in a favor from my younger brother, Stone. I asked him to cook us an elegant meal, and while he was at it, I stopped by the house to see how things were going. As soon as I came in, I smelled fresh bread baking. "Smells great in here, bro."

"Glad you think so." He came out of the kitchen, wiping his hands on a white towel that was hanging from the waist of his jeans. "I'm just about to finish wrapping the asparagus bundles. Come on, you can check out what I've done so far."

Not only was my brother great at cooking, but he knew how to decorate for a romantic evening as well. He led me out to the patio, where he'd set up a small table for two. Paper lanterns hung around the area, waiting to be lit just before nightfall. "Nice, Stone."

The wine was chilling in a stainless-steel bucket, and soft music was already wafting through the air. "I like to get the mood and ambiance flowing well before the actual dinner date begins. But enough about that. Did you pick it up already?"

With a nod, I took the box out of my pocket. "Yes, I did." I flipped the lid open. "What do you think?"

"Holy shit!" His eyes grew to the size of saucers. "That's huge!"

"She's so minimalistic. And I love that about her. But I want her to have at least one glamorous thing to call her own." I put it back into my pocket. "I'm gonna go put it in my bedroom for now. Did the delivery come for her yet?"

"The dress is hanging in her bathroom. And the flowers will be here soon. If you think this looks good now, wait until you see it with red roses everywhere."

My cell rang. "It's Anastasia from work. I bet they've arrived." I answered the call, "Are they there?"

"They are. I've managed to get them up to her suite without her seeing any of them. Once Miss Madison gets here from school, I'll pick her up from the daycare and take her to them."

"She's going to be so excited. She hasn't seen them in a month. I'll call Ember and tell her that I picked Madison up and have already brought her home, so she won't go to the daycare and screw this whole thing up by asking too many questions. Thanks, Anastasia."

"So, *she* came too?" Stone asked.

"Yes, *she* did. When I called to ask her to come, she wasn't into the idea at first. When I told her what I was planning, she said that it was too soon. I told her that I would do it anyway, that it wasn't too soon at all for me since I've waited seven years for this. She finally agreed to come and wished me luck."

"That was big of her." Stone smiled as he shook his head. "I don't know if I would be as nice to any of my exes if they told me they were about to…"

I held up my hand. "Hold that thought. I've gotta get a few more things to set up before Ember gets home." Hurrying to my bedroom, I put the box on top of my dresser, then pulled a bag out of the closet.

I'd made a purchase for Ember that I wanted her to wear underneath the dress I'd gotten for her. Everything came from one of Austin's most upscale boutiques.

I headed to her bathroom to place the clothes in there, wanting to make sure everything looked perfect. I'd bought a tube of red lipstick to leave a little note for her once she got home.

Writing on the mirror over the vanity, I gave her the instructions. *Get dressed, then meet me on the patio. XXOO.*

My heart raced as I went to get ready, hoping that Ember would be on the same page as me. I couldn't be absolutely sure of it, but I had a good feeling about things.

A couple of hours later, I heard her coming down the hallway. The sound of her bedroom door closing had me leaving my room to hurry to the patio to wait for her.

Stone had put the final touches on everything. Red roses filled every nook and cranny. The music was at the perfect level, blending nicely with the sound of the waterfall. The sun, low in the sky now, made the last moment of light the most beautiful.

I filled our glasses with red wine, then stood to one side to hide myself from view. I wanted to witness her reaction.

I didn't have to wait long for her to come out of the patio door. The red dress hugged her waist and held her breasts in a way that took my breath away. Her eyes moved all around the place. "What is happening here?"

I stepped out from behind the bush. "*We* are happening. You and me. Just you and me."

"I thought you had Madison with you." She looked around as if looking for her.

"She's not here. Don't worry, though. She's at the resort with your parents and Ashe and her family. I invited them over for the weekend." I went to her, taking her hand then pulling her close to me. "I wanted to be alone with you."

I held her close enough that I could feel her heart racing. "Alone?"

Leaning in close, I whispered, "Alone." Swaying to the music, I kissed the spot just behind her ear and felt her body sag in my arms as her knees turned weak.

Just like the good old days.

"What's gotten into you, Cohen?"

I twirled her in a small circle, holding her tight. "Stone has prepared dinner for us. Are you hungry?"

Her eyes shined as she nodded. "I could eat."

"Good." I led her to the small table, then pulled the lid off the tray of oysters on a bed of ice. "I thought we might whet our appetite with some of these."

She looked at the platter, then back at me. "So, you want to begin a new chapter for us tonight. One with romance. And since you've provided an aphrodisiac, can I assume some lovemaking as well?"

"Not tonight." I kissed the tip of her nose. Pulling out the chair for her, I helped her sit down, then went to sit down on the chair across from her. "The new chapter part is something you got right, though. And romance will follow. Hopefully."

"Hopefully?" A clueless expression told me she really had no idea what I had planned.

Picking up an oyster shell, I held it to her lips. "Open up."

A sexy smile came my way, then she opened her mouth, and the oyster slipped over her tongue and down her throat. "Yum. It's been a long time since I've had these."

"Last time was with me, huh?" I ate one too.

"It was." She put her hand on mine as I reached for another one to feed it to her. "If there's not going to be any lovemaking, then you shouldn't give me another one of those. I'm having a heck of a time keeping my clothes on as it is."

"So, you *are* still attracted to me then." I had to laugh.

"I know what it's like to become a new parent. Even if you've just become the parent of a six-year-old and not a newborn, it takes a lot of adjusting. I'm not surprised that we haven't had any time for romance. But I'm guessing that's what this is all about."

"Sort of." I took her hand in mine, pulling it to my lips. "Ember, raising our daughter together has shown me so many more reasons to love you. I want you to know that I respect you in every way. I think you're amazing. And I honestly cannot see me living a life that doesn't have you in it."

"Cohen, I have to tell you that I respect you in every way too. You've stepped up to the challenge of parenting like a champ. I had no idea you had it in you. Letting me live here with you so we can raise Madison together has been the most selfless thing I can think of. I can't thank you enough for all you've done. And I can't think about a life that doesn't have you in it either."

"I am glad to hear you say that, Ember." I knew the time had come. Taking the box out of my pocket, I got out of my chair and down on one knee in front of her.

Her hands flew to cover her mouth. "Cohen!"

Opening the box, I showed her the ring. "Ember Wilson, I've loved you since our first kiss. I might not have understood what I felt back then, but I do now. Will you do me the great honor of marrying me and making me the happiest man on the face of Earth?"

She didn't move. She didn't blink. Her chest didn't rise or fall, and I was worried she wasn't even breathing. Finally, she reached out and ran her fingertip over the diamond. "You know, with this gorgeous piece of art on my finger, I'm going to need to up my fashion game. That's going to make Madison very happy. And when she hears that her momma and daddy are going to get married, she's gonna be over the moon."

"Is that a yes?" I had to hear the words.

"Yes. Yes, I will marry you, Cohen Nash. I love you, and I would love to be your wife."

Finally!

EPILOGUE

EMBER

Looking at the ring on my finger, I knew without a doubt that my life was about to change even more. What I didn't realise was how fast it was going to happen.

After I'd accepted the proposal, we ate the meal Cohen's brother had prepared for us. And he kept sending texts to someone every few minutes while we were eating.

"What are you doing?" I asked after a while.

"Just letting people know what's up." He looked at my plate as I placed the napkin on it. "Finished?"

"I'm stuffed. The shrimp bisque and the lobster were filling. I'll have to be sure to thank Stone for this." I reached for the glass of wine only to have Cohen take my hand.

"Time to go." He pulled me up and led me through the house out to the garage. Then, he opened the passenger door of his truck for me.

I saw my purse on the seat, but I had no idea how it had gotten there. "Cohen, how…"

"I'll tell you all about it on our way to the airport." He helped me get in, and then, for some reason, we were off towards the airport.

As we drove there, Cohen remained silent. Instead, he took

a few texts, but he still didn't say a thing. I hadn't noticed the bags in the back until we got out of the truck at the airport, parking on the tarmac near his company's private jet. "When did you pack these?"

"I'll tell you on the plane." He led me up the stairs as another man came in behind us, bringing our things with him. He stowed them underneath a seat then went to the cockpit. "Here, let me buckle your seatbelt."

"Cohen, where are we going?"

After clicking the seatbelt, he put his on too, and then I heard the plane's engine coming to life. "Well, you said yes, so we're going to get married."

"Now?" I couldn't believe it. "Right now?"

"Yes, right now. We'll be in Vegas soon, and then we'll be married before you know it."

"You know, I might want some time to think about this."

"You want to marry me, don't you?"

"I do."

"Cool. Then just sit back and relax. Soon we will be man and wife."

"Cohen, I meant that I want some time to think about a wedding! That's a big deal for me. And I know Madison will be so mad at us for sneaking off and getting married without her present." She was our biggest fan. I knew she would want to be part of the wedding.

"She's not going to be mad." He held my hand then laid his head back. "We should rest now. It's gonna be a busy night."

I had no idea just how true his words were. When we landed, a limo picked us up. As soon as we pulled up to a small church, I started getting a clearer picture of what was happening.

There they were — every member of both of our families. And our daughter stood right in the middle, a bouquet of red roses in her little hands. "Wow." That was all I could say.

"Thank you very much, baby." He got out, pulling me with him. "She said yes!" He held our clasped hands up, and our families cheered.

"Way to go, Momma!" Madison shouted. "I'm ready to be your flower girl." She walked up to me and handed me the bouquet. "These are for you to carry when you walk down the aisle." She took her father's hand. "Come on, Daddy, let's get inside and wait for her to come."

Cohen looked at me before we walked away. "You *are* going to come down the aisle, right?"

I just laughed. "Get out of here, you romantic genius."

Ashe and my father came up to me as everyone else went inside. Dad looped his arm through mine. "You ready, honey?"

Ashe nodded before I could say anything. "I can see it in her eyes. She's more than ready." Holding up her smaller bouquet of red roses, she smiled. "I'll be your maid of honor."

"Are you sure about that?"

"I am extremely sure, sister. Come on, let's get you married off to the man of your dreams."

The next few minutes were a blur of smiling faces. We repeated some words after the Elvis-preacher. And then everything went from blurs to fireworks as Cohen kissed me for the first time in seven years.

My feet felt as if they were suspended in the air, lifted off the floor, and my heart felt heavy, so full of love for him. When our mouths parted, he rested his forehead against mine. "You know, for as much as we kept telling each other that we shouldn't rush anything, we sure have rushed a hell of a lot."

Madison came up between us, grinning as she said, "I just hope you two hurry up and give me a baby brother or sister."

Cocking one brow at me, Cohen said, "I'm game if you are."

Having a baby was a big deal. He had no idea what went into that. And there were just some things that couldn't be rushed. But then I saw our little girl's face all lit up like a sparkler as she waited for me to say something.

So, I tossed the bouquet back over my shoulder and listened to the single ladies clambering to catch it. "Oh, what the heck," I said. "I'm game too, babe." I ran my hand over our daughter's dark hair. "We'll do our best for you, baby girl."

"That's all I ask."

COHEN

Rolling over, I pulled her on top of me. Her breasts heaved as she tried to catch her breath. I gave her no time to do so, pulling her down so I could kiss her.

She was my wife now. I knew I'd done the right thing for once, waiting until we were married to make love to her again. Now that we were man and wife, I saw no end in sight to the lovemaking.

She wrenched her mouth away from mine. "I need some water, Cohen."

Climbing off me, she stood beside the bed, naked as the day she was born. She was drenched in sweat and looked more beautiful than I remembered. "Damn, you're sexy."

She gulped down an entire bottle of water. "And you are insatiable. We have two weeks on this honeymoon. What am I in for? Two weeks of non-stop sex?"

"If you're lucky." I was only kidding. We had travel plans too. I hopped out of bed and got myself a bottle of water. "A hydration break does make sense."

Sitting on the bed, she stretched a bit. "I know we told Madison that we would try to give her a sibling, but I don't think she meant for us to try so hard. We've been at it all night.

We have to face the fact that it might take more than a couple of weeks to give her what she wants."

"Nonsense. We made her in like two seconds. Anyway, we've got seven years to catch up on." I was just joking around, but the look on her face told me she didn't get my joke. "Honey, come on. I'm kidding." I downed the water, then wiggled my fingers at her. "Come with me. Let's take a nice long bath, then we'll go to sleep."

"Yes, that sounds amazing." She followed me willingly, and in no time, we were lying under a blanket of bubbles.

Running my hands over her shoulders, I couldn't seem to get enough of her. Her skin was softer than I remembered. And her body had better curves. I'd had the girl before, and now that I had the woman, I was pumped to go exploring.

But she was tired, and I knew that as she rested her back against my chest. "I can't believe this. We're married, Cohen. My *sister* was my maid of honor. Not in a million years did I see things going this way."

"It just goes to show that you never know for sure what can happen." I kissed a line along her neck. "I'm not upset that so much time has passed, though. If I'm being honest, I needed time to grow up. I needed time to become the man you and Maddy need me to be."

She rolled over, facing me. Her hands moved back and forth slowly on my cock. "I'm glad things fell into place for us when they did."

"I thought you wanted some rest, baby."

Her attention hadn't gone unnoticed, and my cock grew in size with each stroke she made. "Um, not so much anymore. I can't seem to get enough of you, hubby. I think I just needed to rehydrate, is all."

"My little love-monkey." I lifted her, then slid her body down mine until we were connected. "One of the things that makes me happiest about finding you again and finding out that we have a kid is that I get to share everything with you both. I want to give you and our kids the world, baby. I want you to know that neither of you will ever go without a damn thing."

"All I want is your love, Cohen. The money is just a perk. If you had nothing, I would still love you." She moved slowly, making me ache for her to move faster.

"Are you sure about that?" I'd been broke before, and she'd left me. "Did me having money help you make some of your decisions about me this time around?"

"Not really." Running her tongue up my neck, she nipped my earlobe. "I mean, do I like living in a gorgeous home? Well, sure I do. And our daughter seems to have been made for money, the little bougie diva. But, if I'm being honest — and that's all I intend to be for the rest of my days – I didn't make any decisions based on the amount of money or nice things you have. I love you, and that's what mattered most."

"And that's it?" I inhaled quickly as she made some crazy move that sent a wave of pleasure straight through me. "Oh, baby!"

"You like that? I just thought I'd move a little to the left then come back quickly to see what happened." Placing her hands on my chest, she moved up and down. "You make me feel sexy, and that makes me want to try things I wouldn't have had the guts to do before. I think that's why you and I connected right from the start. I felt like I could just be me whenever I was with you. And I felt like you were comfortable enough with me for you to be yourself, instead of Mr. God's Gift to Women Everywhere."

"For the record, I never thought I was God's gift to women everywhere." I laughed. "Just Texas."

Smacking me in the arm, she made the little move again, and this time, she did it twice, igniting a reaction that sent both of us into a tizzy of ecstasy.

The sound of our pants echoed off the tiled walls, and then she laid her head against my chest. "Now, I need sleep."

I kissed the top of her head. "Now, I've got all I need. You, our daughter, and a future that's overflowing with love. Baby, I think we've found it."

"Found what, babe?"

"Our happily ever after, of course."

The End.